Ashley stared at the back of Len's head.

She had a strong urge to run the tip of her finger along the fuzz at the base of his neck. Somehow, its softness didn't fit with the thick muscles that stood out on either side of his neck. But maybe he's not such a tough guy after all, she thought, even if he did come from New York City. And . . . just maybe he could become interested in someone like me.

She fantasized about Len asking her to the homecoming dance, coming up in just two short weeks. Excitement gathered in a tight hot ball in her throat.

Was it so impossible?

Eileen Goudge's Swept Away

GONE WITH THE WISH

#1

Written by Eileen Goudge

Created by Eileen Goudge

AN AVON FLARE BOOK

SWEPT AWAY #1: GONE WITH THE WISH is an original publication of Avon Books. This work has never before appeared in book form.

AVON BOOKS
A division of
The Hearst Corporation
1790 Broadway
New York, New York 10019

Copyright © 1986 by Eileen Goudge Zuckerman
Published by arrangement with Eileen Goudge
Library of Congress Catalog Card Number: 86-90909
ISBN: 0-380-75128-3

First Flare Printing: September 1986

FLARE TRADEMARK REG. U.S. PAT. OFF. AND IN
OTHER COUNTRIES, MARCA REGISTRADA, HECHO EN U.S.A.

Printed in the U.S.A.

K-R 10 9 8 7 6 5 4 3 2 1

GONE WITH THE WISH

Chapter One

ASHLEY STARED AT THE BACK OF LEN CASSI-
nerio's head.

Funny, she thought. Why is it I never noticed before
how fascinating the back of someone's head can be?

Ever since Len had transferred into her history class,
she'd stopped gazing out the window. Watching the squir-
rels chase one another up the big mulberry tree outside
didn't compare with what was right in front of her.

Len's hair was the color of toasted almonds. It was full
and wavy, narrowing to a point at the back where his neck
began. There, the hair grew in a downy line, like the fuzz
on her pale gold angora sweater.

Ashley had a strong urge to run the tip of her finger
along that streak of fuzz. Somehow its softness didn't fit
with the thick muscles that stood out on either side of his
neck. But maybe he's not such a tough guy after all, she
thought, even if he did come from New York City. And
. . . just maybe he could become interested in someone
like me.

She fantasized about Len asking her to the Homecoming
Dance, coming up in just two short weeks. Excitement
gathered in a tight hot ball in her throat. Was it so impossible?

Forget it, she told herself. He doesn't even know you're
alive half the time.

Len leaned forward to scribble something in his notebook. A tear in the seam of his rumpled gray O. Henry

1

High sweatshirt gaped open, revealing a patch of tanned shoulder. What would happen if she wiggled her finger through that hole? He would have to pay attention to her then, wouldn't he?

Ashley sighed, nibbling on the eraser at the end of her pencil. Another girl might have gotten away with it. But she didn't know how to flirt. The last time she'd tried, she'd ended up spilling spaghetti all over the front of Jordan Zimmerman's Lacoste sweater in the cafeteria. That was last year, and she hadn't had the nerve to try again since.

It was incredible, really, when you thought about it. She came from a long line of Southern belles for whom flirting was second nature. Take her mother, for instance. Ashley had seen Mom flirt her way out of any number of sticky situations. All she had to do was flutter those long eyelashes of hers, and men melted.

As for me, Ashley thought glumly, I haven't inherited one smidgeon of Mom's charms. I don't even have the nerve to talk to Len Cassinerio, let alone bat my eyes at him.

If people knew how I felt about Len, they would laugh out loud. Len is only the most exciting thing to hit Westdale since the time Robert Redford's car broke down on Route 46 and had to be towed to the town center to be fixed. And me—I'm just Ashley Calhoun, plain old average Ashley, the Velveeta cheese of O. Henry High. Why, if it weren't for this stupid red hair and the fact that I'm such a klutz, I'd probably melt right into the walls!

Ashley tried to focus her gaze on a patch of blackboard visible between Len's left shoulder and Malcolm Thurston III's briefcase, propped open on his desk in its usual place. Inside the briefcase lay a neat row of pens and pencils, a monogrammed eyeglass case, and notebooks, color-coded according to subject. Poor Malcolm! He was the indisputable king of nerddom. At least, thought Ashley, I'm not like that, thank goodness.

Feeling a little better, she concentrated on the dates Mrs. Killington had scribbled on the board in her neat, cramped hand. She was droning on and on about the Civil War . . . something about Fort Sumter.

"Nothing like an eyewitness report," muttered J.C. McClosky, O. Henry High's junior-class clown, who was sitting on Ashley's right.

Ashley stifled a giggle. All the kids secretly joked that the reason old Mrs. Killington taught history was that she knew it all from firsthand experience. Ashley would never forget the cartoon J.C. had sketched for the school paper. Above the caption "Mrs. Killington's condo" was a drawing of an Egyptian mummy case.

Right now the history teacher sat behind her World War II vintage desk, as erect as if her spine had been replaced by a ruler, arms folded in front of her. Below a helmet of gray hair, a pair of reading glasses anchored by a chain were perched on the end of her skinny nose. Every so often she would nod, and the glasses would slide right off and fall with a flat little bounce against her bony chest.

Bore . . . boring . . . bored, Ashley conjugated in her mind. History was easily her worst subject. Yet her own family history fascinated her. She could dream for hours about what plantation life must have been like for her ancestors around the time of the Civil War. Oh, well, maybe it was just Mrs. Killington. She could make anything boring, even the plot of a Steven Spielberg movie.

What a drag this class is! Ashley thought. I could think of a hundred better ways to spend forty minutes. Starting with my computer. If only I were home now, I could be working my program . . .

Ashley itched to have her hands on her computer's keyboard. To be watching those glowing green symbols—as incomprehensible as hieroglyphics to anyone who wasn't as crazy about computers as she was—scrolling up the terminal's screen. Ashley *never* got bored when she was working on her computer. She loved computerese the way

3

her best friend, Lou Greenspan, loved sixties music. That's why she'd nicknamed her computer Merlin. There was something magic about the things she could make Merlin do. Sometimes she didn't even understand it. It was a lot like a wizard waving his magic wand.

Right now, she thought, if I could make Merlin do anything, I'd write a program that would make Len Cassinerio fall in love with me.

Ashley had been crazy about him ever since that first day he arrived at O. Henry, a transfer student from New York. He'd sauntered into the classroom wearing jeans and an Army surplus flak jacket with the sleeves cut off, looking a little like Rambo checking in for his next mission. She'd felt a tingle of excitement, which turned to instant crush when Len, his dark liquid eyes sparkling with amusement, said, "Yo, everybody . . . I'm Len. What's happening?" Pow! Love at first sight. At least on Ashley's part.

What if she could press the right combination of keys on Merlin and make Len feel the same way about her? But that was impossible—programming a computer to make someone fall in love with you. You'd better stick to the program you're trying to write now, Ashley told herself. It's complicated enough.

Most people would probably think that the program she was working on now was something right out of *Star Wars*. Fourth-dimensional fractals. She'd once tried to explain it to Lou, who viewed anything invented past 1969 with suspicion.

"You know what a hologram is, right?" Ashley had asked as they pedaled their bikes home from school one day the week before.

"Sure, a three-dimensional projection," Lou had said, her chubby face pink with exertion. "One time my parents took me to a museum in New York City that had loads of those. It was like looking at slides, only they weren't flat. You walk all the way around them and see them from any angle. I remember there was this one of a chocolate eclair.

4

It looked so real my mouth was watering! Just don't ask me how they did it."

Ashley had been so caught up in her explanation she'd nearly steered her bike into a fire hydrant. Veering to avoid it at the last possible second, she blew out a deep breath, then said, "Yeah, well, the program I'm working on is kind of like making a hologram, only a step further. Instead of projecting an image that's three-dimensional, I want to do it in four dimensions. *And time is the fourth dimension.*"

Lou shot her a funny look. "Sounds like the Twilight Zone to me."

"It's actually pretty simple. You see, according to Einstein," Ashley explained in plain English, "time doesn't move in a straight line. It's more like a book. Even after you've finished, you can always turn the pages back to the beginning. So just think of the past as a fat encyclopedia sitting on some dusty library shelf, waiting to be checked out." She grinned. "By me."

Theoretically, time travel was possible. But so far no one had ever been able to prove it.

Now the equation for the program tickled at the back of Ashley's mind. It was both frustrating and fun, like groping for a word to fit a crossword puzzle. She had the feeling that if she could just get that last part of the program right, *she* might be the one to prove it.

As she thought about it, excitement skittered in her stomach like a caged squirrel. What if she really could do it?

People would say she was dreaming, of course. How could a sixteen-year-old kid accomplish what the world's greatest scientific minds had been unable to? But what was it someone had said? That the reason kids are often capable of genius is because they haven't yet learned to draw boundaries.

Ashley smiled. Why are you always reaching for the moon, Ashley Calhoun? she scolded herself. Why can't you start with ordinary things—like getting a conversation going with Len, for starters? But why would Len bother talking to someone he probably thought was a number-one, primo klutzo?

Ashley winced at the memory of her graceful entrance to the classroom exactly one week after Len's arrival. She'd been late and had come flying through the door like O. Henry's star running back, Buck Warren, making a touchdown.

Unfortunately, the floor had been waxed the night before. And she'd been wearing a pair of brand-new, slippery-soled loafers.

It was worse than simply falling.

She'd skidded halfway across the room, arms and legs flailing, books and papers flying everywhere, and had crash-landed into a row of empty desks with a horrendous clatter that caused frail old Mrs. Killington to let out a shriek of alarm.

But that wasn't the worst of it.

The worst part of all was that she hadn't even been hurt. Not a scratch! At least, if she'd been carried out on a stretcher, people would've had to feel sorry for her. Maybe Len would have sent her a get-well card. Or visited her in the hospital. That might even have made the whole ordeal worth it.

As it was, she'd had no choice but to pick herself up and face the snickers of the whole class. Ashley's cheeks burned at the memory of Len's amused grin.

"Yo, Ashley . . . way to go!" he'd said, giving her a thumbs-up sign as she slunk past him to her seat.

Ashley had wondered if it would be possible for her to hide out in her locker for the next five months and twenty-two days of her junior year.

Ashley was picturing trying to cram her lanky frame into a locker when she was interrupted by a tap on her shoulder.

She twisted around in her seat, knocking her history book with her elbow. She grabbed for it as it slid off the desktop, managing to catch it before it hit the floor. Whew, that was close!

She let out her breath and looked up to see Alicia Sanchez, at the desk behind hers, holding a scarlet-tipped finger to her pursed lips.

"Sshhh," Alicia whispered. "This isn't a public announcement." She slid a folded slip of notepaper into Ashley's hand with a sly wink. "Pass it up to Len, will-ya?"

Ashley felt as if she'd been handed a tarantula. Alicia writing notes to Len meant she was interested in him. Of course, what girl in her right mind wouldn't be?

The difference with Alicia was that she stood a very good chance of getting him.

Alicia, with her melted-chocolate hair and amber cat-shaped eyes. Alicia, who had a body Jane Fonda would envy. Plus, she knew how to use it. Ashley and her friends had often joked that Alicia should have a road sign posted on her: DANGER, CURVES AHEAD.

Now it looked as if Len was about to be added to Alicia's casualty list.

Ashley felt her whole body sag. Silly. How could I ever have thought, even for ten seconds, that I might have a chance with Len?

Unlike Alicia, when Ashley wore a tight sweater it was only because she'd accidentally shrunk it in the wash. Like the one she had on now. Her favorite angora sweater, which was now two sizes too small.

As Ashley reached to pass the note to Len, the folded paper fluttered open. "Meet me after class." It was signed simply "A."

Just as she'd thought. Alicia definitely had something going with Len. They were beyond first names. They were down to initials already. He probably knew her phone number by heart.

The notepaper seemed to burn into her fingertips. Ashley dropped it quickly over Len's shoulder as if it were

7

on fire. Please don't turn around, she begged him silently.

She didn't want him to see her disappointment. She was sure her feelings were all over her face like a blinking neon sign.

Oh, no! He's turning around. He's looking straight at me! Why is he smiling that way?

Realization struck like an avalanche. Oh, my gosh! How could I be so dense? That "A." He thinks *I* sent the note. Why didn't I realize before I passed it up to him?

What a fool! All this time, hoping and praying Len would turn around and smile at her. But not like this. Not because of a *mistake*. He was probably laughing at her. What a joke, the classroom klutz making a play for O. Henry High's resident hunk, right?

Ashley forced a sick smile in return. Her cheeks grew even hotter as Len winked at her before turning back to face the front of the room. A bubble formed in her chest and floated up into her throat. She hiccupped softly. Why do I always get the hiccups when I'm upset? she agonized. I'm hopeless. Really and truly hopeless.

She took a deep breath and began counting to ten. One, two, three, four—

The bell rang on the count of five. Air exploded from her lungs. She had to get away quickly. Len might get to her before Alicia got to him. She'd be forced to explain that it was all a mistake. But how could she talk to him with every other word a hiccup? She'd only make an even bigger fool of herself.

Ashley scooped her books into an untidy pile, tucking them under her arm as she ran. Blood pounded in her cheeks as she wove her way between desks, heading for the door. She brushed past the radiator, hissing steam at her, past the ancient slide projector, crouched like a bulldog against the back wall, its thick black cord snaking along the yellowing linoleum tiles, waiting to trip her. She concentrated so hard on avoiding it, she almost *did* trip over it, but with a little skip regained her balance.

8

Ashley escaped out the door into the corridor and attempted to lose herself in the crowd that was gathering in front of the lockers.

"Yo . . . Ashley!" A familiar voice floated above the student babble.

Heads turned. People stared. Ashley ducked down, wishing she could disappear. This stupid mop of hers was like waving a red flag. And now she had a face to match!

Ashley was edging toward the mass of bodies surging down the stairwell when a locker flew open in her face. She stopped suddenly, and was immediately rear-ended. Someone muttered "I'm sorry," but it was too late. Ashley lurched, and lost her balance. Books and papers slithered to the floor. Horror washed through her in an icy flood.

Oh no, not *again.*

Amid a tangle of Nikes and Reeboks, she sank to her knees and began scooping the mess into a pile. Out of the corner of her eye, she spotted a pair of faded denim pant legs making their way toward her. Len! How could she face him now? This was the ultimate. Dead-end City. The chance of him ever seeing her as anything but a klutz was less than zero.

She looked up just in time to see Len waylaid by a dusky arm decorated to the elbow with a rainbow of rubber bracelets. Alicia. As she leaned close to Len to say something, their heads nearly touched, and her long shimmering hair slid seductively in front of her face like a veil.

Ashley felt as if she were scooping her insides up off the floor as well. She quickly stood up, clutching a messy pile of books and papers, and made a dash for the stairwell. She knew she should really thank Alicia for getting her off the hook as far as talking to Len was concerned, but she still felt terrible. Tears of humiliation and jealousy stung her eyes.

She was no match for Alicia Sanchez. If they posted a

road sign on me, Ashley thought, it would read: WATCH OUT FOR FALLING ROCKS.

"Did you ever hear this one?" Lou Greenspan thumbed the dial on her car tape deck to turn up the volume. "It's by Creedence Clearwater Revival."

Ashley stared out the window as Lou's vintage Volkswagen bug rattled along Longfellow Road. Once upon a time, somebody had gotten tired of naming roads after trees, she reflected absently. So half the roads in Westdale were named after poets and authors. Other than that, Westdale was just an ordinary New England town. White-frame colonial-style houses slid past on either side, bordered by lawns so green and perfectly maintained you could have used them for billiard tables. Ashley had lived in Westdale all her life, so she knew the whole town inside and out.

Someday, she wished, just once, I'd like to live someplace else. Someplace where everybody doesn't know that my father owns Conn-Tech Computers. And no one could remark about what an adorable baby I used to be. Or remember that I broke my ankle climbing the church steeple to rescue a bird's nest when I was nine.

"Ashley?" Lou's voice broke into her thoughts above the loud music.

"Huh?"

"Don't tell me you don't know who Creedence Clearwater is?" Lou sounded as shocked as someone else might be if she were talking about Bruce Springsteen.

Ashley gave an apologetic shrug. "Sorry. Hey, could you turn it down a little? Loud noise always gives me a headache."

"Noise? You call this noise? 'Bad Moon Rising' is one of the greatest songs ever written!"

Ashley looked over at her best friend and laughed. Lou's round face wore an expression of utter outrage. She narrowed her big blue eyes. Then, sticking her lower lip out as far as it would go, Lou blew an exasperated breath upward, scrambling the blond curls that cork-screwed down over her eyebrow. Even so, her stocky frame—cloaked in the Oshkosh overalls that had been her uniform since the age of two—continued to bounce to the beat of the music.

"Face it, Lou." Ashley giggled. "Even though we were both born in the same year, you've been going backward ever since, while I've been going forward. Honestly, I don't see the big attraction of the sixties."

Lou sighed. "I must be some kind of a throwback. Did I tell you I dreamed I met Bob Dylan last night? I offered him half my Moon Pie in exchange for his autograph." She took a bite out of the Moon Pie on the dashboard, still half-wrapped in its silver foil. An expression of pure bliss floated over her face. She offered it to Ashley. "Want some?"

Ashley shook her head. "No, thanks." Her stomach was still clenched into a knot after what had happened earlier that afternoon.

"It's weird, isn't it? I mean, my parents must be the only people who went through the sixties without learning how to macramé or tie-dye a T-shirt. I'll bet they've never even *heard* of brown rice."

"What does brown rice have to do with it?" Ashley asked.

"Everything! Back in the sixties, everybody was a flower child. And they all had long hair, and ate brown rice, and listened to the Jefferson Airplane."

"Jefferson who?"

Lou blew out another exasperated breath. "Grace Slick's old band. Except now it's Jefferson Starship, with only a few of the same musicians. But that's still not the point. What I'm trying to say is, I must be some kind of delayed reaction. You know, all that sixties stuff bounced right off my parents and onto me."

Ashley nodded, holding back the smile that twitched at the corners of her mouth. "Makes sense."

Lou turned off Longfellow Road onto Emerson Avenue

11

with a *cha-clunk* of gears. Here, the lawns were broader and lusher, the houses larger and set farther back from the road. This was Ashley's neighborhood.

"Oh, what's the use of trying to explain it?" Lou sighed, taking another bite from her Moon Pie. "No one understands. They all think I'm some kind of a freak. Especially boys. Remember the time I went out with Boomer Franklin? He attacked me, and then acted surprised when I pushed him away. He said he thought all hippies were into free love."

"Don't worry, Lou"—Ashley patted the plump hand on the steering wheel—"I love you, anyway . . . even if I don't share your taste in music. Besides," she added with a sigh, "generation gap isn't the only handicap as far as striking out with boys goes. They're not exactly falling all over themselves to get at me either, you know. In fact, today it was the other way around . . ."

Lou, who had known Ashley since kindergarten, didn't have to be told the gory details. "Uh-oh. Not again."

Ashley reflected that she was probably the only kid in elementary school who had brought Band-Aids to school in her lunch pail. It seemed like Lou had always been there to help her put them on . . . and peel them off. And wasn't it Lou, in the sixth grade, who had managed to unhook Ashley's braces from Mary Sue Cunningham's sweater without tearing it after the two of them got stuck together playing tag ball? Ashley practically owed her life to Lou Greenspan.

Ashley nodded, the humiliation of sixth period washing over her again. "It was awful. Everyone was watching. I was trying to get away fast so I wouldn't have to talk to Len. Then I dropped my books all over the place. Talk about two left feet! Len probably thinks I have three of them. He wouldn't ask me to the Homecoming Dance now if I were the only girl at O. Henry."

"What I don't understand is why you were trying to run away from Len in the first place," Lou said. "Last week,

12

you were down in the dumps because he *wasn't* paying any attention to you.''

"It's a long story. Trust me, you don't want to hear it."

"Oh, Ash"—Lou took one hand off the wheel to pat Ashley's head—"you know it's all up there, don't you? You're not really so clumsy. Or at least you wouldn't be if you didn't *think* you were.''

"Okay, I just imagined the whole thing."

Lou pulled up the long drive to Ashley's house. From the road, no one would even know there was a house hidden behind all those trees. That's how Ashley felt about herself. It was like being in disguise. If what Lou was saying was true, somewhere deep down in this gawky body of hers there was a graceful butterfly waiting to emerge.

"I didn't say you imagined it," Lou protested. "What I meant was, it's like when someone tells you not to think about elephants. You're so busy telling yourself *not* to trip over things that you wind up doing it. Maybe if you just learned to relax a little . . . Hey, have you ever tried meditation?''

"You mean like sitting cross-legged on the floor and chanting while you burn incense?" A tiny gleam of amusement forced its way through the black cloud that hung over Ashley's head.

Lou giggled. "Okay, I know it sounds silly. It was just a thought. I even tried it once myself.''

"What happened?"

"Nothing. It only lasted about thirty seconds. I couldn't sit still any longer than that. Besides, incense makes me sneeze.''

They both laughed, and Ashley felt better.

Up ahead, through the trees, a pair of gleaming white columns peeked like a pair of old-fashioned pantaloons from under a wide ruffled skirt. At least that's how her mother had once described it, and the image had stuck in Ashley's mind ever since. Now the trees parted and the rest of the house came into view—three stories of colonial red brick festooned with ivy and wisteria. The white columns on either side of the porch didn't really belong, in Ashley's opinion, but the way Daddy told the story, Mom had fallen in love with the house years ago before they bought it. She was terribly homesick after they moved north, and those pillars reminded her of Georgia.

"Oh, Ash," Lou said after the VW had shuddered to a stop in front of the pillars. Her round blue eyes were serious for once. "You're such a terrific person. You're the only one who can't see it."

"What about Len . . . does he need glasses, too?" Usually joking helped. But right now she was just too depressed.

"Ash, it has to come from inside you first. Then Len will see it. You know you're really pretty. I've always envied your red hair. A lot of people have carrot-colored hair, but yours is really red. And think how many girls our age would kill to be as skinny as you. Remember that time I borrowed one of your swimsuits? I couldn't get it up past my ankles!"

Lou laughed good-naturedly. Being a little on the chubby side didn't bother her, at least not enough to give up Moon Pies and go on a diet. She liked the way she looked, even if it wasn't perfect. Ashley envied her for that. She'd be happy to trade some of her skinniness for a good-sized chunk of Lou's confidence.

"Thanks, Lou," Ashley said. "I appreciate what you're saying. But you're my best friend. If best friends didn't say nice things about each other, they wouldn't be best friends."

"Okay." Lou tossed up her hands. "Don't believe me, then. I guess you'll just have to look in the mirror for the truth next time."

Ashley opened her door. "You want to come in for a while? I wasn't planning on doing anything special except work on my computer program."

"No, thanks, I want to drop by Uncle Joe's record store.

He promised he'd get me the Beatles' original *Sgt. Pepper's Lonely Hearts Club Band* album. I want to see if it's come in yet.''

Lou had been weaned on sixties music by her uncle, who owned a music store in town called Pounds of Sounds. He was always getting special albums for her, and when the two of them got together, they could talk rock trivia for hours on end. The last time Ashley had tried joining in on one of their conversations, she'd felt like she was in outer space, struggling to understand some kind of weird Martian dialect. The same way Lou claimed to feel about her computer lingo.

Ashley wasn't too disappointed as she watched Lou drive off, honking a few farewell beeps on the ancient VW's horn. She loved spending time with Lou, but right now she was anxious to work on her fractal program.

Standing on the front porch, Ashley closed her eyes for an instant and imagined she really could go back in time. She'd never let the fantasy get this far before. Where, out of all the eras to choose from, would she go?

She leaned back against a pillar. Of course! It was the most obvious choice of all. She would go back to Oakehurst in the nineteenth century, before the Civil War. That was the plantation her great-great-grandmother had lived on. Ashley had heard any number of stories about Violet Oakes, whose portrait had been handed down through the generations and now hung over the fireplace in Ashley's living room.

But the only image it conjured in Ashley's mind was the scene from *Gone with the Wind* where Scarlett goes charging across the lawn, ruffled skirts held high, with Tara looming in the background.

Gone with the Wind was Mom's favorite movie. In fact, she'd named Ashley after one of its characters. It didn't matter to her that it was a boy's name. Now it seemed to Ashley that it must have been an omen. Mom had somehow known even back then that there was nothing very feminine about her daughter.

But real life at Oakehurst couldn't have been like a movie. It was probably a lot duller. People sitting around on verandas fanning themselves and sipping mint juleps for hours on end.

Anyway, it doesn't really matter, she told herself, because I'm never going to find out. Spying on people who lived over a century ago is just a silly fantasy, like wishing Len would fall in love with me.

Ashley straightened, shaking her head as if to clear it. You might as well face facts, Ashley Calhoun. You're doomed to remain a twentieth-century klutz.

Chapter Two

"ASH, HONEY . . . WATCH OUT FOR THE DOOR frame!" her mother called from somewhere in the house as Ashley came in through the front entrance. "I just had it touched up, and the paint's still . . ."

" . . . wet," Ashley supplied with a groan, staring down in disgust at the streak of dark blue paint on her favorite white jeans. Nice going, klutzo.

She found her mother out on the sun porch, pruning the Boston ferns. This was Ashley's favorite room in the whole house. Sun poured through the glass panels all year round. And when she was lying on the couch looking straight up through the glass roof, she almost felt as if she were outside, watching clouds chase each other and birds build their nests in the overhanging trees. Her mom, who had a real talent for decorating, had done it all in white wicker, with bright floral cushions. And there were so many plants it was like being inside a terrarium.

"Oh, Ashley." Eugenie stared at Ashley's pants in dismay. "I guess I should have warned you a little sooner."

"It wouldn't have mattered," Ashley said with a sigh. "Things like wet paint and gum on the sidewalk have a way of attaching themselves to me no matter what. I guess I must be some sort of human magnet for disaster."

Eugenie set her plant shears down on a little wicker table. "Well, I'll admit you went through your awkward stage, but I thought that was all over. You're a young lady now. And a young lady . . . Well, I don't know exactly

17

how to put it, honey. But do you think you could try being a bit more delicate?''

Delicate. The word teetered in Ashley's brain like a china teacup on the verge of crashing to the floor. Mom is so graceful and delicate, she thought, it's hard to believe I'm not adopted. Chewing gum wouldn't dare stick on her shoe. And if she ever ran into a lamppost it would only be because the lamppost had been rude enough to step in her way.

Ashley stared at her mother, despair welling up inside her. If only I *could* be delicate like Mom! But that's impossible. For starters, we don't look anything alike. Mom is petite and dainty. Her hair is honey-colored, not flaming red. And her eyes are blue, with long lashes that don't need a speck of mascara. Mine are muddy brown, and as far as the rest of me goes . . . well, it's pretty much hopeless.

But Ashley kept her frustration to herself. ''I'll try, Mom,'' was all she said. There was no use trying to explain. Mothers refused to accept the truth about their kids. It was built into their hormones or something. I could have three left feet, and Mom would still insist I had the potential to be a ballerina.

''I suppose it's partly my fault.'' Mom still had the soft slur of a Southern accent, and pronounced ''I'' as ''Ah.'' ''You were such a tomboy. I nearly had to wrestle you to the floor to get you into a dress. But I should have insisted more often. Which reminds me, I was in Brigitte's today, and there was this perfectly adorable dress in exactly your size. I bought it for you. It's on your bed.''

Eugenie smiled, pleased with herself. As if the solution to all Ashley's problems were as simple as buying the right dress. She raised a small hand with polished pink nails to her throat, fingering the cameo brooch pinned to the neck of her ruffled Laura Ashley blouse. The brooch had been in her family for generations. It had belonged to her great-grandmother Violet. For Ashley it was just one more painful reminder of all the decades of family tradition she could never hope to measure up to.

"Thanks, Mom." Ashley was grateful for her mother's thoughtfulness, but she knew without looking at it that she wouldn't like the dress. Mom always picked out dainty, ruffled things that would look wonderful on *her*, forgetting the fact that she'd given birth to a gangly giraffe.

"I thought you could wear it to the picnic tomorrow." Eugenie picked up her shears and began snipping at a fern.

Ashley flopped down on the wicker couch. "I hear it might rain." She tried not to sound too hopeful as she stared up at the thickening clouds overhead. But the picnic was definitely not something she was looking forward to.

Every September her father gave a picnic for the employees of Conn-Tech. Indian summer lasted until the beginning of October, so usually the weather was nice. Everybody ate outside on the grassy slopes of the town green. Afterward they played softball. Last year Ashley was shortstop on her father's team. She'd struck out more times than anyone else. The last time with the bases loaded and the score tied in the final inning.

This year she was about to strike out again. Len would be at the picnic. His father was one of Conn-Tech's engineers. How could she face him again after what had happened this afternoon? Next time it would be Len running in the other direction!

"Bite your tongue," Mom scolded. "The picnic hasn't been rained out once in twelve years, and it's not going to be tomorrow."

Of course, Ashley thought. It wouldn't dare rain on Eugenie Beaumont Calhoun. "Just my luck," she muttered.

"What, sugar?" Eugenie turned to Ashley with a questioning look, holding a limp yellow frond as gingerly as if it were a lace fan.

"Oh, nothing." She rose from the couch. "I'm going upstairs to work on my computer program." At least there was one area where she was on sure ground.

Eugenie gave a tinkling laugh. "You and that computer. I do declare, Ashley, when y'all are fooling around with that thing, it's like you're off in another world."

19

Mom, you have no idea how close you are to being right, Ashley answered silently. The thought perked her up, and she galloped halfway to the staircase before she remembered her promise to her mother. She slowed as she was crossing the front parlor. Staring down at her feet, she forced herself to take small mincing steps. But the flowery swirls in the Oriental carpet made her dizzy, and it seemed to take forever to get to the other side of the room.

This is crazy, Ashley thought. I'll never be Scarlett O'Hara. Why am I wasting my time doing this?

Then she thought about Len. Maybe Mom was right. If she made a real effort to be more "delicate," Len might forget to notice her gawkiness. Learning to take tiny steps might even make her look smaller.

Ashley grabbed an enormous dictionary from the library shelf. It had to weigh at least thirty pounds. Yes, this would do. She balanced it on top of her head and began slowly retracing her steps. One, two, three . . . don't think about striking out. Four, five, six. . . . think about Len instead . . .

An image of Len and Alicia, their heads bent together, popped into her mind.

The dictionary slithered to the carpet with a dull thunk.

Ashley groaned, bending down in exasperation to pick it up. It had opened to the D's, and one of the definitions seemed to leap out at her.

Disjointed (adj.) 1. out of joint 2. disconnected; without unity or coherence.

That described her all right. Disconnected. The fuse that connected her brain to her body had blown.

Ashley had the sudden feeling she wasn't alone. Glancing up, she found a pair of merry brown eyes gazing down at her from the portrait of Violet Beaumont that hung over the fireplace. Violet almost seemed to be laughing at her.

"I'll bet you're wondering how I could possibly be related to you," Ashley said aloud to Violet. "Grandma

Beaumont told me you had more boyfriends than any other girl in the state of Georgia. And I can't even manage to get one." She closed the dictionary with a snap. "Too bad you can't talk. Maybe you could show me how you did it."

Violet hadn't been all that beautiful, in Ashley's opinion. Her features were ordinary, except for her flaming red hair, which no one else in the family had had the bad luck to inherit except me, Ashley thought. But she had had something else—a sparkle that came through even in this painted portrait. It was in her eyes, and in the saucy tilt of her mouth, which seemed to hint at secrets untold.

Ashley stared hard at the portrait as if she could somehow divine those secrets. Violet looked as if she had been about Ashley's age when it was painted. She wore a brilliant purple blue ballgown that showed off her minuscule waist and creamy shoulders. Her hair was parted in the middle and gathered into two bouquets of finger curls on either side of her head. In one dainty hand she clutched a lacy handkerchief, half-hidden in the folds of her skirt.

Oh, well, Ashley said to herself. Whatever secrets Violet is hiding, she's not going to pass them on to her great-great-granddaughter. But it doesn't really matter. They'd probably be wasted on me, anyhow.

She returned the dictionary to its shelf and continued taking small steps all the way up to her room, where she collapsed in a sprawl across the foot of her four-poster bed. In the privacy of her bedroom, she could be as klutzy as she wanted.

Something hard was poking her in the foot. Ashley sat up and saw that a big red box marked "Brigitte's" sat propped against one pillow. She pushed it aside with her toe, feeling guilty for not appreciating Mom's present more. She would try the dress on later.

Right now, more exciting things awaited her. She gazed across the room at the computer that occupied the surface of her antique rolltop desk. Merlin. He stared back like an unblinking eye, his blank screen shimmering with a faint green phosphorescence. Almost as if he were beckoning her.

Ashley's depression lifted. Excitement began to seep in. Secrets. Merlin had his secrets, too. All she had to do was find the right key to unlock them.

Drawn as if by a magnet, Ashley went over to her desk and sat down in front of her computer. She had built Merlin herself, bit by bit, byte by byte, over the past two years, using everything from components salvaged from other computers to the latest inventions of Conn-Tech's research division. It was like no other computer she knew of. That was why she'd named it Merlin, making "it" a "he." She and Merlin were old friends now. Ashley patted it affectionately.

Last summer she had read an article in the *Journal of Science and Mathematics* about experiments being done powering computers with light instead of electricity—using photons instead of electrons. The idea ignited her with such excitement that she'd spent half the summer developing a photon power unit for Merlin, which, as she'd explained to Lou in the simplest of terms, was sort of a high-tech light bulb. Now Merlin was able to roam far beyond the binary logic that limited most computers. That was how she'd been able to develop her fractal program.

Or, as she would have explained it to Lou, she had invented what could quite possibly turn out to be a modern-day version of H. G. Wells's time machine.

Ashley flicked a series of switches, and Merlin blinked on with a reassuring beep.

Ashley smiled. "Hello to you too, Merlin." She moved the cursor down and began tapping on the keyboard. A string of glowing green numbers and symbols jumped to life on the screen.

There was no way she could have explained how her program worked, because she didn't fully understand it herself. All she knew for sure was that a fractal was a portion of something. In this case, a portion of the fourth dimension. And the fourth dimension was time.

A weird pulsing blob began taking shape on Merlin's screen. It was sort of like watching an amoeba under a microscope, Ashley thought. Excitement skittered in her stomach. So far this blob had appeared every time she worked on her fractal program. But she hadn't been able to get beyond it.

She smiled to think what Lou's reaction would be. Psychedelic! Far-out!

She frowned. But something was wrong. It wasn't far-out enough. The program wasn't working the way it should.

Ashley wasn't sure what she expected. In the movies, wild-eyed professors got into weird contraptions that looked like souped-up telephone booths, and after they'd pulled some levers and cranked a few dials they climbed out into another century. But what on earth could you expect from a computer?

Maybe the past would appear on the screen like a video-tape on a VCR, she reflected. Wow, wouldn't that be neat! I could watch things that happened hundreds of years ago just like a movie. That would sure beat Mrs. Killington's boring lectures. I could get straight A's, and I'd never have to crack a book!

As if absorbing her excitement, the blob on the screen began to pulse faster.

Then Ashley remembered something. The laser gun. Conn-Tech's newest miracle. They hadn't finished ironing out the glitches, but Dad had brought it home anyway for Ashley to try. Connected to a computer, it was supposedly capable of projecting three-dimensional holographic images. But so far it hadn't worked very well in the Conn-Tech lab. Ashley suspected there was nothing wrong with the laser gun. It was the computers they were using that were at fault. They weren't fast enough or smart enough.

But Merlin was.

What if she could use the laser gun to turn that blob into a hologram and project it right off the screen? What would happen?

There was only one way to find out.

Ashley got up and removed the laser gun from its plastic carrying case. Her heart beat rapidly with anticipation. In a way, she felt sort of silly. Like when she was a little kid and used to pretend she was Captain Kirk beaming up to the *Starship Enterprise*. Even so, she couldn't help thinking this was how Einstein must have felt when he discovered how to smash atoms. Oh, boy, was she going to have something wild to tell Lou tomorrow if this worked!

She spent over an hour fitting the laser gun to Merlin's connectors, and was almost finished when a boom of thunder startled her into nearly dropping the gun. Lightning ignited Ashley's room with a flash of stark brightness, followed by a sudden torrent of rain.

Ashley felt an irrational surge of panic. Was the storm some kind of omen? There was always a thunderstorm when creepy things happened in the movies.

She looked about her room, storing it away in her memory as if she might never see it again. The four-poster bed with its colorful crocheted spread. The macramé wall hanging Lou had made her, which she loved even though it clashed horribly with the English garden wallpaper. Her ancient stuffed teddy bear, Boo-Boo, slouching on the window seat, his one remaining button eye seemingly fixed on Merlin with a wary expression.

What if she went away and never saw any of it again?

But that's ridiculous, she told herself. Why should I feel as if I'm going somewhere? This isn't the *Starship Enterprise*, for heaven's sake! I'm in boring old Westdale, where nothing exciting ever happens. And great scientists don't walk around with books on their heads. Even if I do get this thing to work, it'll probably just make some neat pictures. Like a three-dimensional slide show, or something.

Ashley took a deep breath to stop the fluttering in her stomach.

And switched on the laser gun.

At first nothing happened.

The blob on Merlin's screen was still just a blob. It pulsed and shimmered and . . .

. . . and it was growing!

No. It had to be her imagination. But the blob continued to grow until it had filled the whole screen. It *couldn't* grow any more, unless . . .

It's growing right off the screen.

Ashley's mouth went dry. Her heart pounded with excitement and terror. Wow, oh wow . . . Lou's never going to believe *this!*

The blob had become a great mass that engulfed her entirely. It swelled until it was big enough for two people to fit inside. All around her, sparkles of light shimmered and swirled like a slow-motion cyclone. The numbers and symbols that filled Merlin's screen scrolled upward—faster and faster—until they were a flickering blur of iridescent green.

Ashley felt dizzy. And she was *seeing* things. Even stranger things than this weird cocoon of light. A second ago she could have sworn she glimpsed an old-fashioned ship sail right across her carpet. And there . . . over by her bed. One of the posts was sprouting leaves!

Ashley squeezed her eyes shut. This can't really be happening, she told herself. I'm imagining this. I've been fooling around with this program so long I'm losing my marbles. Okay, I'm going to take a deep breath and count to three. And when I open my eyes again, everything will be back to normal.

One . . . two . . . three . . .

Ashley opened her eyes and gasped.

An armor-clad knight on a black horse came charging through the wall, his lance pointed straight at her.

She lunged for the switch to shut Merlin off just as the knight faded into the opposite wall.

Still unable to believe that what she was seeing wasn't some weird hallucination, Ashley looked down at her hand. A scream of horror stuck in her dry throat. Her hand was nearly transparent. She could see right through it!

A wild breathless excitement swept through her. Had she done it? Had she really stumbled through the door of time?

But where was Merlin taking her? Would she ever be able to come back?

"Wait!" she cried. It was all happening too quickly. She wasn't ready.

Ashley tried to turn Merlin off, but it was too late. Her hand passed right through the switch.

"Help!" Her cry seemed to echo as if from the bottom of a deep canyon.

The lights were spinning faster now.

She was no longer in her bedroom. She was . . .

Oh, God, I don't know *where* I am.

"Somebody . . . help me!" she cried again. But this time it was like screaming something out the window of a speeding car. The words were snatched from her mouth by some sort of crazy slipstream.

A rushing sound filled her ears. The walls had disappeared and she was surrounded by shifting images. A stone hut with a thatched roof. Two little Indian girls crouched before a fire. A man in a white toga running past them . . .

Ashley felt herself spinning helplessly. The rushing sound in her ears grew louder. And she realized it was the pounding of her own heart. She had never been so scared in her whole life.

I'm lost, she thought.

I'm lost somewhere in time!

Chapter Three

KA-BOOM!

A sound like a falling tree echoed deafeningly in Ashley's ears.

It was followed by a flash of blinding white light.

Ashley squeezed her eyes shut. She was too terrified even to scream. She felt as if she'd been spinning through outer space and had collided with the sun.

She groped wildly for something, anything, to hang on to. Her fingers closed over something smooth and hard. Abruptly, the spinning sensation stopped.

Silence. The rushing sound had stopped, too.

Ashley was scared to see where she'd landed. Or when. If her guess was right, if she *had* opened the door to time, then she could be anywhere. Medieval England. Or Ancient Greece. Or even back in prehistoric times. A tyrannosaurus could be on the verge of gobbling her up at this very moment . . .

The thought caused her eyes to fly open.

Ashley let out a startled gasp.

She was right back where she'd started. In her room, her hand clutching one leg of her oak night table. And everything was exactly the same as it had been before she plugged in the laser gun.

A tidal wave of relief washed over her.

There was her bed, with the big red box from Brigitte's right where she'd left it on the pillow. The door to her closet—known as the "compost heap"—was open just as it had been, the floor a swamp of inside-out jeans, crumpled sweaters, and balled-up socks. What a wonderful sight! She would never clean it up. She would leave it that way forever. A monument to ordinariness.

Feeling slightly hysterical in her relief, Ashley leaped from her chair with a wild giggle and dashed over to the window seat, scooping Boo-Boo into her arms. She hugged him, his button eye pressing into her cheek.

"Oh, Boo-Boo," she cried, "I was so scared. I didn't know if I was ever coming back."

Outside, rain rattled against the window. Thunder pounded like a hollow drumbeat. Lightning slashed the cloud-dark sky.

How *did* I get back, she wondered.

She stared at Merlin as if her computer could supply her with an answer. The screen was blank. No glowing symbols. No blinking cursor. Somehow, it had gotten turned off. Then Ashley noticed the light over her desk was off as well. And she remembered turning it on when she sat down to fiddle with her program.

Of course! The storm had knocked out the electricity. It happened all the time around here during thunderstorms.

Along with comprehension, excitement began to seep in, replacing her panic.

If shutting Merlin off could bring me back, then I can control this time thing. I can go back and forth in time whenever I want.

The realization brought waves of dizziness that rocked her like the aftershock of a dynamite blast.

"Do you know what this means?" she cried, holding Boo-Boo out and shaking him so that his head flopped to one side, giving him a quizzical look as he peered up at her with one startled eye. "I did it! I really did it! I found a way to travel back in time!"

Me, Ashley Calhoun of boring old Westdale, Connecticut. The klutz of O. Henry High. The disjointed daughter of Eugenie Beaumont Calhoun.

I did what none of the world's great scientific minds

28

have ever been able to do. Even if I still don't know exactly how.

What if it had been an accident, something she'd merely stumbled on? Well, she was certainly klutzy enough for something like that.

Another wild giggle escaped her. I'm no ordinary klutz, she thought. I'm a *cosmic* klutz.

But whether it had been an accident or not, she was stuck with the inescapable fact that she'd performed some sort of miracle.

Where do I go from here? she asked herself. Her heart was still beating like crazy, but she was thinking more clearly now.

As if in answer to her thoughts, the light over her desk blinked on again. Merlin let out a frantic-sounding beep, and onto its blank screen popped the glowing green message: *Program interrupted. Please try again.*

Should I? Ashley wondered. Still clutching Boo-Boo, she approached Merlin as if he might bite.

"What if I can't get back the next time?" she asked Merlin. "Did you ever think of that?"

Beep-beep, Merlin replied as she pushed the keys that would reactivate the program.

"You think you're so smart," Ashley continued. "But you're only man-made, and what's out there is . . . well, really spacey. I'm talking heavy-duty *Star Wars* stuff, Merlin."

The program began scrolling up onto the screen. And that gave Ashley an idea.

What if I adjusted it so that I could go back in time to one specific place? Then I wouldn't be floating around in that . . . that cosmic garbage disposal out there. And while I was at it, I could fix it so I'd only be gone a few minutes. Just enough to see if it worked. And then later on when I got braver, I could go back for longer periods.

Ashley set the digital timer to allow herself exactly two minutes before Merlin would shut off, automatically returning her to the present.

Now, where should I go? she asked herself. It was a mind-boggling prospect, choosing a time to return to. But she didn't have to think too hard about it. She'd always wanted to go back to Oakehurst, her great-great-grandmother's plantation in the South. It was one of her most cherished fantasies. But she figured she would need a little help in pinpointing it.

How would Merlin know where Oakehurst was?

Then suddenly she realized she'd overlooked the most obvious tool of all. Of course! She could tap into the public library's computerized resources with her modem. It was so simple. All she had to do was dial a special code number on the telephone that would hook her modem into the library's computer, and all that historical data would be at Merlin's fingertips.

She grabbed the phone on the small table beside her desk and began excitedly punching out her code. A second code connected her with the library's system. Then she dropped the phone's receiver into the special cradle by Merlin's side, through which the information could be fed to him.

Following another series of commands, she entered: *Destination: Oakehurst, Georgia, 1861.*

For some reason the year 1861 seemed significant. She wasn't sure why. Maybe it had something to do with Mrs. Killington's lecture on the Civil War.

She tapped the control key: EXECUTE.

That weird jellyfish blob appeared once again. It expanded until it had filled the entire screen with its pulsing luminescence.

Now, for the moment of truth.

Ashley switched on the laser gun. But as the blob began oozing off the screen, she jumped up from her chair, leaving her teddy bear in her place. Phase one of the experiment: Use a volunteer so you don't have to be the guinea pig.

"Sorry, Boo-Boo," she said as the holographic blob slowly engulfed him, "but I have a lot more to lose than you do."

30

An image of Len Cassinerio's face floated into her mind. Those dark Rambo eyes seemed to be watching the experiment, too. The corner of his mouth curled up in a sultry smile.

"Way to go, Ashley," he said.

What would Len say if he could really see this? Wouldn't he be impressed? Maybe he would decide she wasn't as hopeless as he'd first thought. And when she was called aside in class to be told she'd been nominated for the Nobel Prize, Len would give her the thumbs-up signal. Only this time he wouldn't be joking.

But no, she couldn't tell Len or anybody about this. Not for a while. What if the wrong person found out? She'd seen an episode of *Star Trek* where someone went back in time and changed the entire course of history. Germany won World War II and ended up taking over the world. She couldn't let something like that happen.

So for now, it had to remain a secret.

Ashley held her breath as she watched Boo-Boo and the chair he was sitting on fade slowly into the swirling cocoon of light. Good-bye, Boo. Don't take it too hard. You'll be back. I hope.

The mist evaporated, leaving only a faint greenish glow in the empty space where it had been.

The next two minutes seemed to stretch like hours. Ashley's stomach felt like the heavy-duty cycle on a washing machine gone haywire. She strode back and forth across her raspberry-colored shag rug, too excited to stay in one place.

The first thing she did as she paced the room was to lock her bedroom door. Mom would have a heart attack if she walked in when Boo-Boo returned. How would she ever explain it? Hey, Mom, I'm practicing this neat magic act for the school talent show—what do you think?

Next, for something to do while she was waiting, Ashley went over to her bed and opened the package from Brigitte's. Pink ruffles cascaded over the cardboard box. She lifted it out and held it up to her. Yuck. It wasn't that the

31

sundress was all that horrible, but it belonged on someone else. Pink, with her red hair, made her look like a lit birthday candle. And ruffles definitely weren't her thing.

So now I'm stuck deciding whether to not wear it and hurt Mom's feelings, or wear it and make an even bigger fool of myself in front of Len.

Ashley caught herself and laughed. This was crazy. How could she stand here worrying about a dumb dress when Boo-Boo, the time-traveling bear, was about to make history?

As if in response to her thought, the mist began to take shape again in the middle of her room. Ashley jumped a little, and felt the dress slide through her frozen fingers onto the floor.

Where was Boo-Boo?

Then she saw the outline of a chair glimmering in the mist like a connect-the-dots drawing. Slowly, it began taking shape. Boo-Boo, too.

Ashley ran over and snatched him up as soon as he was all there. He felt warm, as if he'd been sitting in the sun. But he was definitely the same cock-eyed Boo-Boo, lumps, missing patches of fuzz, and all.

She hugged him. "If only you could talk. I'll bet you saw some things out there that would knock the socks off Winnie-the-Pooh."

Her whole body blazed with a mixture of excitement and terror. Now that the experiment with Boo-Boo had been successful, it was time to try it herself.

What would she find if she went to Oakehurst? What strange things would she see? Would she catch a glimpse of Violet Oakes Beaumont?

All she had to do to find out was allow herself to be swallowed by that shimmering holograph . . . and be swept back in time.

Ashley rechecked the bedroom door to make sure it was still locked. Then she positioned herself in front of Merlin. She was sweating like crazy. Even the tips of her fingers felt slippery as she moved them over the keyboard, reactivating the program.

Wow, am I nervous, she thought as the blob bloomed off the screen, enfolding her in its petals of mist. It's exciting, but gosh, how scary, too. Is this how the Wright Brothers felt the first time they got their plane off the ground?

She managed a tiny smile. Well, maybe one of these days I can ask them myself how they felt.

Before she even knew what she was doing, Ashley began to sing. Lou claimed singing aloud when you were scared was a good way of making yourself feel better. For Ashley, it was a way of assuring herself she was still there, even while she felt herself fade into nothingness.

She pushed back at the panic crowding in on her. Okay, but you got yourself into this one on purpose, Ashley Calhoun. So just sit back and fasten your seat belt. It's too late to change your mind now.

The rushing sound filled her ears, and the walls of her room slowly evaporated. It was as if the whirling mist had become a tunnel, and she was being sucked along through it. Currents of air beat at her like the flapping wings of a hundred birds. She had a weightless feeling, as if she were floating. Her voice became an echo. No, a thousand echoes, like a chorus of angels singing.

"Oh, I wish I were in Dixie, hurray, hurray . . ."

Chapter Four

"WHOA . . . WHOA THERE, BEAUJOLAIS!" A young man's voice commanded above the clattering of hooves.

Huh? Where on earth—

Abruptly, the swirling mist was gone, and Ashley found herself standing in the middle of a country road surrounded by fields. A great gray-speckled horse was galloping straight at her. A few feet away, it reared up as its rider reined it in, struggling to bring it under control.

Ashley's mind spun with panic. I'll be trampled if I don't get out of the way!

But her body was ignoring the frantic signals her brain was telegraphing to it. The air seemed to be made of the marshmallow-creme filling in Lou's Moon Pies, making each movement sticky and sluggish.

It was as if she'd awakened from a dream . . . only to find herself in this other dream. She tingled all over, like when an arm or a leg that had gone to sleep was waking up, only it was her whole body.

Is this really happening? Or am I imagining it?

The horse continued to dance and whinny before her. She felt its flank brush her shoulder as it wheeled around. The strong grassy smell of its lather filled her nostrils. And the loud exclamation of its rider was no dream. She had never heard anyone speak that way, so how could she have dreamt it?

"God's knickers!" he swore when he'd finally managed

to calm his mount. "Don't you know enough to jump out of the road when you see someone coming? Boys with nothing better to do than idle about getting in the way ought to be horsewhipped!" He spoke with a strong Southern accent, every word dipped in molasses.

Ashley felt as if he'd dumped a bucket of cold water over her. "I'm not a boy!" she shot back, forgetting her confusion for an instant. "And—and I'm sorry I didn't get out of the way. But I—I didn't see you coming."

The person atop the horse stopped swearing and stared down at her in surprise.

Ashley stared back.

She had never seen anyone dressed the way he was. Not in real life, anyway. Only in the movies and in illustrated history books. He wore a pair of mustard-colored breeches—that's what they were called, wasn't it, those pants that ended at the knees?—and a ruffled shirt under a dark brown jacket with gold buttons. A gleaming black stovepipe hat perched atop his sleek dark head.

He looked as if he'd stepped from another century.

No, she corrected herself, *I'm* the one from another century.

Realization hit her like the sonic boom after a plane has passed overhead.

Holy moly, I've really done it! I must be back in Oakehurst!

Suddenly, for no reason at all, she began to giggle. "I—I'm sorry. I don't mean to laugh. But you look so funny . . . in that hat."

"Funny?" His eyebrows drew together.

For the first time, Ashley noticed what color his eyes were. Blue. His hair was very dark and shiny, like patent-leather dress shoes. He reminded her a little of Rhett Butler, only a lot younger. Probably not much older than she was.

"That hat makes you look like Abe Lincoln," Ashley struggled to explain.

Instantly, she could see she'd said the wrong thing.

35

"God's knickers!" he roared so loudly his horse whinnied and began dancing about again, its hooves raising little puffs of dust. "Only a Yank—" He caught himself and abruptly broke into a startled laugh. "Well, you're not a boy, and you're clearly no Southerner . . . Why, y'all must be Miss Leonore Beaumont from up North. Violet said you'd be arriving any day, but I declare I never expected anything like this!"

Ashley felt herself go hot as she looked down at herself, suddenly seeing herself the way he did. In her jeans and sweater, no wonder he'd mistaken her for a boy! And not a very well-dressed one, either, judging from his much more refined outfit. And to think she'd laughed at *him* for looking strange. She had to remember who was the fish out of water here.

He leaped down off his horse. In a single motion, he swept his hat off his head and bowed low before her. "Allow me to introduce myself, Miss Beaumont. Brett Hathaway. My folks's plantation is up yonder. Lilac Hill." He pointed up the road, but Ashley saw no sign of either a hill or lilacs. All around her were nothing but fields of cotton and plowed red clay. He turned back to Ashley. "I beg your pardon for speaking so roughly in front of a lady like yourself just now, but I—I thought . . ." Brett's voice trailed off in embarrassment. "Well, never mind what I thought. It wasn't just Beau you spooked. I thought I'd seen a ghost when you popped up like that out of . . . well, out of *nowhere,* it seemed like. But I must have imagined it. The heat, you know." He drew a handkerchief from his pocket and mopped his forehead. "But now that I know who you are—Say, perhaps your brother spoke of me to you? We met when he was down from Harvard visiting your cousins at Twin Ridge."

Her brother? This was crazy! How could he possibly know Andy? Besides, Andy was away at Brown University—

She caught herself. Oh, he must mean Leonore's brother. But who on earth is Leonore Beaumont?

36

Then Ashley remembered that Beaumont was Violet's last name. Violet had married a man named Elliot Beaumont. Or at least she *would* marry Elliot if she hadn't already. Leonore had to be Elliot's sister.

Ashley struggled to recall what she knew about Elliot Beaumont. It wasn't much. Most of the stories she'd heard from Mom and Grandma were about Violet. She'd been a regular firebrand, according to Grandma. A real-life Scarlett O'Hara, who in some ways was years ahead of her time. Ashley's favorite story was about how Violet had shocked the entire county by refusing to ride her horse sidesaddle, as all ladies were expected to.

All she knew about Elliot Beaumont was that he'd been a big Union hero, and that he and Violet had had six children.

There had never been any mention of a Leonore Beaumont.

Why does Brett think I'm she? Ashley wondered.

"Miss Beaumont?" Brett was looking at her strangely again.

Ashley realized she'd drifted off again. It was so weird, thinking of yourself in one time . . . and being in another. It was the feeling she sometimes had walking out of a movie theater, with half her mind still wrapped up in the movie and the other half trying not to step in the muck on the sidewalk.

"I—I'm sorry," she stammered. "The heat. I guess I'm just not used to it. I felt a little faint for a minute."

She fanned herself with her hand. It *was* awfully hot. In fact, it was positively *broiling*. She could have used a little bit of that rain she'd left behind in Westdale.

"Well, I declare," Brett said, sounding nearly as confused as she felt. "It's no wonder, you traipsing about without a bonnet in this sun. I don't mean to be rude, Miss Beaumont, but I just can't keep from asking—whyever are you dressed that way? I've heard you Yankees have some mighty strange habits, but this sure does take all!"

Ashley didn't know what to say. Her dazed mind turned

cartwheels, struggling to think up some sort of excuse. Why hadn't she planned this out more? She'd gone on Girl Scout camping trips better prepared than this!

She ended up telling the truth, because she couldn't think of a lie. "I like these clothes. They're comfortable."

Brett's eyebrows shot up in amusement. "I declare, you are the strangest girl I've ever met. But I suppose it makes sense when you look at it that way. If you're going to go gallivanting about like a field hand, you might as well be dressed like one." He caught himself, and a hint of red crept into his cheeks. "No offense intended, you understand."

Suddenly it occurred to Ashley that far more than two minutes had passed since she'd arrived in this century. Had something gone wrong with Merlin? Hadn't the timer gone off?

Her heart did a nosedive of terror. Good Lord, she could be stuck here forever!

The prospect was so overwhelmingly scary she started to feel dizzy again. Everything had turned a sick gray color. A swarm of angry hornets buzzed inside her head.

She felt a strong hand grip her elbow. Brett's voice sounded muffled, as if her ears were stuffed with cotton. "You look a mite pale, Miss Beaumont. Are you strong enough to ride in back of me? Lilac Hill isn't far. Just up the bend. And it's nice and cool inside."

Ashley nodded, taking deep breaths until the dizziness subsided. What else could she do but agree? If Merlin didn't hurry up and zap her home, she'd be left standing out here in the middle of nowhere.

Brett Hathaway encircled her waist with both hands, lifting her up onto the back of his horse. Instinctively, Ashley swung her leg over so that she sat astride its rump.

Once again, Brett eyed her as if she'd sprouted two heads. "Never saw a lady sit on a horse like that before," he muttered. "Must be another one of your strange Yankee customs."

"But it's so much easier this way," Ashley blurted, remembering the story about Violet.

Brett only shook his head as he mounted the bay named Beaujolais. But when he glanced back at her, he wore an amused smile.

"You Beaumonts must have a habit of bucking tradition," he remarked as Beaujolais took off at a fast trot. Ashley gripped her legs tighter and held on to his jacket to keep from falling off. She had learned to ride at summer camp and was pretty good at it. But she was a little unsteady at the moment. Brett continued, "Your brother Elliot had some mighty strange ideas, too."

"Oh?" Ashley managed distractedly. Her thoughts were still on Merlin and why the computer hadn't yet returned her to the present. Her insides turned slow somersaults of fear. The program had worked on Boo-Boo, why wasn't it working on her? Was she destined to be marooned in a time way before even her grandparents had been born? Her fingers and toes went numb with icy terror.

Stop! she told herself. Get a grip on yourself, Calhoun. You can't think this way. Eventually someone at home will realize you're missing and figure out how to get you back. Or, more likely, someone will shut Merlin off; then you'll be zapped home automatically.

Relax, she commanded herself. Look around you and enjoy it while it lasts. Okay, so it didn't work out the way you thought it would, but you're not, I repeat *not,* going to be stuck here forever.

She took several deep breaths and willed herself to concentrate on the landscape as Brett Hathaway nudged Beaujolais with his heels into a comfortable trot.

It's unreal, she thought. I've never seen countryside like this. No cars. No road signs. No telephone wires, even. Just row after row of cotton bushes, and this brick-colored dirt.

A jackrabbit bounded across their path, disappearing into the grass that grew high alongside the road. Cicadas whirred in the dusty trees that drooped overhead.

Ashley instinctively searched for signs of the twentieth century—a rusty soda can, an abandoned tire, anything that would prove this was some kind of bizarre charade. Because she still didn't quite believe it was really happening.

Brett's slow-as-molasses drawl jerked her out of her reverie. "You'll pardon me for being presumptuous again, Miss Beaumont. But p'raps you wouldn't mind telling me why you chose to walk from the train station rather than take a carriage? It doesn't make a whole heap of sense to me."

Ashley was stumped again. "Uh . . . I . . . Well, it was such a nice day. And I wanted to stretch my legs after that long, uh, train ride. I guess I didn't realize how far it was."

"Well, pardon me for saying so, but you can't go to Oakehurst looking like that. Lionel Oakes would throw you out on your ear. I reckon you'll have to set a while at Lilac Hill while I send someone for your trunk."

"My trunk?" Oh, yes, people had trunks in those days instead of suitcases. "Uh . . . Well, you can't send for it because . . . because it's lost. When I got off the train, I couldn't find it. Someone must have taken it by mistake."

Brett shrugged. "A pity, but no doubt it'll turn up soon. Don't you fret none. I'm sure one of Lavinia's dresses will fit you. My sister's about your size."

Ashley watched the tips of his ears turn pink at the mention of her size. Goodness, she wondered, what would happen if Alicia Sanchez ever got unleashed on this century?

The thought caused her to smile, and she realized that in spite of her anxiety about returning home she was actually enjoying herself. Brett Hathaway was really very sweet, considering that, as far as he was concerned, she was behaving like a raving looney-tune.

"You're very kind," she murmured, copying his old-fashioned speech.

As long as I'm here, I might as well try acting as if I belong, she decided. Heaven knows when I'll get back home to Westdale.

Or if I *ever* will, she reflected with a sinking heart. But she pushed the frightening thought aside again. Think positive, she reminded herself. Someone will rescue you sooner . . . or later.

"That was plumb close," Brett said a short while later, as they rode toward Oakehurst. Beaujolais had been exchanged for a buggy pulled by a pretty chestnut mare. "If Mama and Sissy had been up from their naps, I sorely doubt we'd have gotten away without a long-winded explanation as to why I saw fit to borrow one of Sissy's dresses."

Ashley looked down at the dress she was wearing. With all the ruffles and billows she was surrounded in, she felt as if she'd stepped into a bubble bath. The top was trimmed with lace and gathered with green velvet ribbons, and the skirt was made of yards and yards of some kind of shiny green-plaid material that lay over more yards of ruffled white petticoat. The waist was a little tight, but she'd managed to close the buttons in back by sucking her stomach in as far as it would go. Now she would just have to figure out a way to keep from breathing for the rest of the trip!

"I'm sorry to put you to so much trouble," Ashley apologized. "You've been awfully nice." She fiddled with the carved handle of the parasol Brett had thoughtfully provided as well to keep the sun off her face.

It sure is hot under all these clothes, Ashley thought. She was starting to sweat. Or maybe it was just Brett's nearness that was making her nervous. She couldn't remember when she'd last sat this close to a boy, except for Len. But the back of Len's head in history class didn't really count, did it?

Unlike Len, who didn't know she was alive except when she was dropping things, Brett was staring at her with real interest.

"Forgive me for being so bold, Miss Beaumont," he said, his cheeks flushing red. "But I couldn't help noticing

41

how captivating you look in that dress. You should always wear green, with that red hair of yours.''

Captivating? Ashley fought the urge to look over her shoulder to see if he was talking to someone else. That was one word she never would have used to describe herself. Except for the time she accidentally locked herself in the bathroom. But that wasn't the kind of captivating Brett had meant.

She felt the heat that had been trapped under her clothes climb up her neck and spread through her cheeks. ''I hope Violet won't be too surprised to see me,'' she said, desperate to change the subject. ''I mean, I did sort of drop in unexpectedly.'' Boy, did she ever!

She was worried about what she was going to say when Violet saw that she wasn't Leonore Beaumont. Would she believe it if I told her the truth? Ashley wondered. No, probably not.

''I wouldn't exactly call your visit unexpected,'' Brett said with a laugh, his square chin tilting back. ''Why, I've heard tell that Violet's been counting the days ever since she got your letter from Philadelphia saying you were coming.''

''Philadelphia?''

''You *do* live with your aunt in Philadelphia, don't you?''

''Uh . . . yes . . . of course.''

''Your brother told me the whole story when he was visiting your cousin's plantation last month. I remembered because it seemed so sad. You both losing your parents that way and having to move up North to live with your aunt. You must get mighty homesick for good old Georgia, living all the way up there.''

''Well, I . . .''

'' 'Course, I can tell it's been a while since you left. You even sound like a Yankee!'' His blush deepened, and he looked down at the reins in his hands. ''If you'll pardon me for saying so.''

''That's okay.'' Ashley smiled. ''I've been called worse

42

things than a Yankee.'' She didn't add that her brother Andy's nickname for her was ''Splashley''—because of all the times she'd spilled her milk at the table.

''In any event, I know that Violet is simply dyin' to meet you,'' Brett added, turning the carriage up a wide, elm-lined avenue that wound up a gently sloping hill. Above the treetops, Ashley glimpsed an enormous white house—much bigger and grander even than Brett's—shimmering against the hot blue sky.

''Meet me?'' Ashley muttered under her breath. Her confused mind scrambled to piece together what Brett was saying with what she already knew.

That means Violet and Leonore have never seen each other, she thought. Violet doesn't even know what her future sister-in-law is supposed to look like. Unless she has a photograph. Have cameras been invented yet? Oh, why didn't I research this period a little better before I went back?

Stop, Ashley told herself. You're jumping ahead of yourself again. Why not just wait and see what happens? If nothing else, you'll finally get to meet your great-great-grandmother. What a trip! Ashley felt the knot of tension inside her give way a little as they drew closer to the house.

She turned her attention to her surroundings, noticing that the dirt road they'd been on had given way to a stone-paved drive surrounded by lush green lawns and flowering bushes. How beautiful! She caught her breath in delight as a peacock wandered out from behind a lilac bush and lazily fanned open his brilliant feathered tail.

The wheels of the carriage rolled to a stop on the stone drive before a wide veranda skirted by massive white columns, each one as thick as two of Ashley. Wisteria vines had crept up over them, their clusters of purple blossoms dangling like bunches of grapes. Bees buzzed, and a heavy sweet scent filled the air.

So this was where my great-great-grandmother Violet Oakes lived! Ashley thought, filled with awe. It's so enormous. And so grand! More like a museum or a fancy hotel than someone's house.

"Wow, this is really neat!" she cried.

"Neat?" Brett laughed. "Of course it's neat. It's kept that way. I declare, Miss Beaumont, you do say the strangest things!"

Ashley bit down hard on her lower lip. How was she supposed to know what to say and how to behave in this century without making a complete fool of herself? It was worse than constantly tripping over her own two feet back in Westdale.

Brett must have sensed her discomfort, because he was quick to ask, "Have I insulted you, Miss Beaumont? I meant no offense. I like a lady who's full of surprises." His blue eyes fixed on her in a way that made her squirm with discomfort.

Was Brett interested in her? she wondered with a jolt of surprise. She honestly couldn't see why. What was even harder to figure out was how she felt about him. Sure, he was handsome enough to push any girl's temperature up a few degrees. And nice, to boot. Yet when you got right down to it, he was over a hundred years older than she was! Wow, she thought, this is all so confusing. I'll have to sort it out later. Right now, I hardly know where my head is at, much less my heart!

An image of Len sauntering into Mrs. Killington's classroom that first day flitted across her mind. Somehow, even though Len wasn't here—in fact, she reminded herself, he hadn't even been born yet—he seemed more real than the flesh-and-blood Brett Hathaway seated beside her.

Ashley's thoughts were interrupted by a sudden crash as the front door flew open and a girl with bright red curls, dressed in a billowing yellow dress, came flying down the wide marble steps of the veranda.

"Leonore! Oh, Leonore, is that you?" the girl cried as she neared the carriage. "My heavens, I thought you'd *never* get here. It's been weeks and weeks since I got your letter. You can't imagine how impatient I've been to meet you!''

"Violet?'' Goosebumps crawled up Ashley's arms as a pair of familiar brown eyes peered up at her. How many times had she seen that face, those laughing eyes, gazing down at her from the portrait over the mantel?

Wow, this is creepy, Ashley thought. It's almost like seeing a ghost! The only difference was that Violet was wearing a yellow-and-white-sprigged dress instead of the purple blue ballgown in the portrait.

And there was certainly nothing ghostlike about Violet, as she practically dragged Ashley down from the carriage and squeezed her until Ashley could have sworn she felt her ribs cracking.

When she'd loosened her wrestler's hold, Violet danced back a step, her wide skirt swaying like a bell. "Let me look at you! I declare, you're not a bit like Elliot described you. He said you were on the plumpish side, and just look at you. You're nothing but skin and bones! And your hair! Elliot didn't tell me you had red hair. Why, it's the very same color as mine.'' She peered closely at Ashley, her head cocked slightly to one side, her amber-colored eyes narrowed with concentration. "It's the most curious thing, but I do believe y'all look more as if you could be *my* sister than Elliot's.''

Ashley let out a sudden startled laugh. "Yes, you and I could be related, couldn't we? Oh, Violet, you have no idea how much I've wanted to meet you, too!''

She wished she could tell Violet the truth but sensed that now wasn't the time. Maybe after they got to know one another better. For the moment she was simply relieved that Violet still believed her to be Leonore. How else could she have explained her presence?

Violet squeezed her hand. "We'll have all the time in the world to get acquainted, dear Leonore. In fact I already feel I know you after all Elliot's told me. And I'm certain it won't be any time at all before we'll feel as if we really are sisters.'' She glanced up at Brett, her heart-shaped face

45

creasing with a frown of consternation. "Oh, dear, I'm afraid I've been most horribly rude. Brett Hathaway, you're simply a darling to have brought Leonore here. Do come in and sit with us and have something cool to drink."

Brett tipped his hat at Violet and said, "Thank you for your gracious offer, but I must be getting back. As far as escorting Miss Beaumont, why, it was my pleasure. We had a most . . . ah . . . interesting ride. I was only sorry I couldn't be of assistance in finding your misplaced trunk, Miss Beaumont . . ."

"Mercy, what a nuisance . . . but never you mind about your trunk," Violet replied, turning to Ashley. "You can wear my things until it turns up. I've plenty of dresses I can't wear anymore, and I'm sure they'll fit you just fine, even if you are a few inches taller than I am."

"Did you outgrow them?" asked Ashley. It was hard to believe. Violet was so dainty. Why, you could practically thread a needle with her waist! Ashley thought.

Violet giggled. "Of course not, silly. It's just that they're last season's gowns, and I've already been seen in them at least twice. I don't know what kind of customs you're used to up North, but around here a girl might as well go wearing homespun clothes as be seen socially in the same dress more than twice."

Ashley smiled to herself. She'd have to try *that* one on Mom sometime.

If I ever find my way home, a little voice inside her head nagged at her. Panic closed a fist about her throat once again. But she struggled against its grip. Someone will rescue me, she thought. Someone *has* to.

Lou! Ashley remembered. She knows about my fractal program, even if she doesn't completely understand it. Lou would certainly try to help . . . if she could.

Ashley forced herself to think about the unthinkable. What would happen if she was wrong, if she couldn't get back? The tightness in her throat became almost choking. But she reminded herself once again that it was too soon

46

to panic. Most likely no one at home had even discovered she was missing.

Besides, it was impossible to stay upset around Violet for very long, she discovered. As soon as Brett had said his good-byes, Violet was dragging Ashley into the house, chattering a mile a minute.

". . . and I want to hear all about your brother, every detail"—she lowered her voice as they approached the open front door, glancing about uneasily—"as soon as we're alone. If I so much as mention Elliot's name around Papa, he turns the most awful shade of purple." For a moment Violet grew serious, and her eyes glimmered with tears. "You might as well know the truth, Leonore. I've been hopelessly in love with your brother ever since he danced with me at your cousin Stuart's ball," she confessed as she led Ashley into an enormous room with sunlight streaming in through tall French windows.

It reminded Ashley of her own parlor back in Westdale, where Violet's portrait hung. But hers seemed dwarf-sized compared to this.

Holy moly! This room is the size of a gymnasium. And look at the furniture—wouldn't Mom go crazy over all these fantastic antiques?

Wait a minute! She caught herself. What am I thinking? Most of this stuff isn't antique yet. It just looks that way to me.

Violet leaned forward and took Ashley's arm. "But Leonore," she whispered solemnly, "Papa would rather die than see me marry Elliot. And I'm certain I'll die if I don't!"

Ashley tried to absorb what Violet was telling her, the awesome room and its furnishings forgotten for the moment. Well, it was no surprise that Violet was in love with Elliot Beaumont. But why would Violet's father be dead set against her marrying him? That didn't make any sense.

"Don't worry," she whispered to Violet. "It'll work out. I *know* it will."

But a terrible thought had just occurred to her. What if,

47

by zapping herself into the past, she'd somehow messed up the way her family history was supposed to turn out? Holy moly, that would mean . . .

. . . Elliot and Violet might *not* get married!

Something even more terrible occurred to Ashley.

Maybe I *won't* get rescued. Maybe that's why I can't get back to my own time—because if Violet and Elliot never got married, then *I* was never born!

Maybe it's up to *me* to find a way to get back, she thought, a wave of terror crashing over her. Maybe the problem doesn't have to do with Merlin or my fractal program after all, but with Violet and Elliot. Could my journey back through time have somehow rearranged history, just like in that *Star Trek* episode? Could I have accidentally messed up the way things are supposed to work out by coming here?

A wave of time-lag dizziness swept over Ashley once again, that weird feeling of being caught between two worlds. She clutched the back of a chair, her fingers closing over polished wood carved in an intricate rose pattern. She took a deep breath. Slowly, the room stopped spinning.

If Violet and Elliot are the key to my getting back, I'd better find out everything I can about them, Ashley reasoned, fighting to keep herself calm.

Not an easy task when your stomach is trying out for the Olympics, she thought despairingly.

Chapter Five

"WHY DOESN'T YOUR FATHER WANT YOU TO marry Elliot?" Ashley whispered. She wondered if it had anything to do with Violet's age. She did seem awfully young to be thinking about marriage.

"Well, it's not so hard to understand, is it?" Violet sighed. With a swish of skirts, she settled onto a massive curved-back sofa covered in wine red velvet and beckoned for Ashley to join her. "Papa gets so terribly violent on the subject of abolition, and Elliot . . . Shhh, I hear Papa coming now." Violet lowered her eyes and began fussing nervously with her lace collar.

Before Ashley could sit down, a tall stern-faced man strode into the room. He had long graying sideburns that covered most of his cheeks, and bushy eyebrows that grew together over the bridge of his hawk nose, giving him a permanent scowl. Ashley instinctively felt afraid of him.

The hand he extended toward Ashley was cool and dry, his handshake brisk. "Welcome to Oakehurst, Miss Beaumont. I hope your stay will be a pleasant one. For all of us," he added, his mouth a grim line of disapproval.

Ashley stared down at the floor, counting the petals scattered on the Oriental carpet under a vase of flowers. What had he meant by those last words? Was he warning her?

Ashley felt as if she were two people. Herself and Leonore Beaumont. While her own mind whirled and dipped with questions about Violet and Elliot as well as her own predicament, she struggled to respond to Violet's father as she supposed Leonore would have.

"Thank you, Mr. Oakes," she replied. "I'm sure it will be."

Papa Oakes's expression softened slightly as he peered at Ashley more closely. "Well, you don't look a whit like your brother." Abruptly, his scowl returned. "I sincerely hope that difference applies to your thinking as well."

Ashley wished she knew what was going on. Why did he hate Elliot so much? This was all so confusing! But before she could say anything else, Papa Oakes turned and strode from the room, his heels clacking against the polished floor with a hard sound that vibrated in the pit of Ashley's stomach.

Red spots of embarrassment stood out on Violet's cheeks like pinch marks as she turned to Ashley. "I must apologize for Papa. He—he's not usually like this. But you see, Elliot"—her small hands fluttered helplessly—"well, they didn't exactly see eye to eye. And Papa can be so stubborn. So can Elliot, for that matter." She brightened, and a mischievous twinkle crept into her eyes. "If I tell you a secret, do you promise not to tell a soul?"

Ashley smiled, remembering her earlier wish to know Violet's secrets. "Believe me, there's no one I could tell even if I wanted to," she said. "And if it's got anything to do with boys, I'm dying to hear it."

Violet gave a startled laugh. "Land sakes, you do say the strangest things, Leonore. Do all Yankees talk like you? I've known only one other person from up North, and he—" She stopped herself, glancing over her shoulder as if her father might still be within earshot. "Come on upstairs. I'll show you my room."

Some things never change, I guess, thought Ashley, amusement pushing its way to the surface of her troubled thoughts. She and her friends always headed straight for their rooms whenever they were over at one another's houses. The really crucial subjects—like whether a certain boy would call or not, or what Clarissa Van Dyke heard

50

him say about you to his best friend, whose girlfriend had a locker next to Clarissa's—just couldn't be discussed in the living room or kitchen.

Ashley followed Violet toward the sweeping marble staircase, trying desperately not to trip on her skirts or bump into something. Getting around in these clothes couldn't be easy even for someone as graceful as Violet, she reflected. For Ashley, it was like picking her way through a minefield dressed in a circus tent.

Something caught her eye—a tall carved secretary against the wall in the hallway—and Ashley halted abruptly. As she moved her hand across the dark polished wood, a lump rose in her throat. It was the very same secretary that sat in the parlor of her house in Westdale!

Once again she had that dizzy sensation of straddling two worlds. She ran her finger down the leg she'd gouged when she rode her tricycle into it at the age of three. Only now it was perfectly smooth. The lump in her throat grew larger, and her eyes filled with tears. Would she make it to the twentieth century, as this desk had?

"What is it, Leonore?" asked Violet, looking concerned.

"Oh, nothing." How could she tell Violet the truth? "I guess I'm just tired. It's been a long day."

"Of course, you poor thing! Land sakes, what a ninny I've been, chattering away like that with you dead on your feet after your tiresome journey. Honestly, Leonore, you must think my manners no better than Papa's! Come on upstairs and I'll loosen your corset for you."

"Corset?"

Violet's amber eyes widened. "You're wearing one, aren't you?"

Ashley shook her head, afraid to say anything that might reveal her ignorance. A corset was some kind of undergarment, wasn't it? Like an old-fashioned bra. She'd read about women wearing them, but she'd never actually seen one.

Violet's eyes widened even further, and she clapped a

51

hand to her mouth as a shocked giggle escaped her. "Why, Leonore Beaumont! It's a wonder you can even button that dress. Nobody I know would *dare* go about in public without a corset."

"Why not?" asked Ashley, feeling a little braver. Now that Violet knew how ignorant she was on the subject of corsets, she had nothing to lose.

"It's—" Violet started to say, then suddenly looked at a loss. "It's just not done, that's all. You're just lucky you're so slender. Anyone else would look like a cow. Besides," she added mysteriously, "it's for a good cause."

Ashley trailed up the stairs behind Violet, trying to copy her mincing steps. "What cause?"

Violet paused to give Ashley a sly wink over her shoulder. "Why, the only cause that matters—men! They like us to appear delicate and on the verge of swooning. Who wouldn't be, laced into a corset so tight you can't breathe?" She laughed. "But they're not supposed to know that. Men can be such silly gooses!"

"Is Elliot like that?" Violet asked.

Violet's smile turned to a frown of bewilderment. "What an odd question—asking me about your own brother."

Ashley felt herself go all hot and prickly. "I meant . . . Well, he might seem like a completely different person to you, that's all."

Violet paused at the first door after they'd reached the landing. "No," she said, "Elliot's not like that. He's more interested in what I think than how I look. I suppose that's what made me fall in love with him. He asked me how I felt about slavery. No one's ever asked me how I felt about *anything.* Certainly not Papa."

"What about your mother?"

Violet blinked. "Didn't Elliot tell you? Mama died when I was just a little girl. Typhoid. I can't even remember a time when it wasn't just me and my brother, Rance, and Papa. Sometimes I get so tired of them ordering me about, I'd like to just—" She stopped herself, looking horrified at

52

her own words. "Mercy, there I go again. Boring you with all my talk."

"I don't think it's boring at all," Ashley said.

"You're sweet, Leonore. Even if you are a bit strange."

Ashley cleared her throat. "There's one thing, Violet. I'd like it if you didn't call me Leonore."

"Land sakes, whyever not? Isn't that your name?"

"Leonore's my first name, but nobody ever calls me that. Mostly I go by my middle name. Ashley." She had worked this lie out in her mind while she was climbing the stairs and hoped it sounded convincing enough.

"What an unusual name. It doesn't sound Southern."

"Oh, it is," Ashley said, struggling to keep from smiling. "In fact, I'm named after a Southern character in a mov— I mean, book. Only you've probably never heard of it."

"You're just like Elliot," said Violet as she opened the door to her room. "I never met anyone who loves books so much. In fact"—she lowered her voice—"he sent me one. That's the secret I was going to tell you."

Ashley didn't see how a book could be a secret, unless it was a sexy book. And she couldn't imagine Elliot sending Violet something like that.

Violet pulled Ashley into the room, locking the door behind her. It was a large room, at least twice the size of Ashley's, with tall windows opening onto a balcony. The sweet scent of lilac and magnolia drifted in, reminding Ashley of the sachets of dried flowers her mother tucked into her drawers to keep her slips and nightgowns smelling fresh. The lump of homesickness in her throat began to ache.

So different, yet so many reminders. Violet's bed was a four-poster like hers, but with a lace canopy to match the lace curtains that fluttered at the windows. Her room even had its own fireplace, only it was smaller than the one downstairs. Over the mantel hung a portrait of a young woman in a powdered wig and colonial dress. Was she any relation to Violet?

Against the opposite wall was a tall carved dresser in which Violet was now rummaging, standing on tiptoe on a needlepoint footstool to reach one of its top drawers. Lacy handkerchiefs and silken underclothes fluttered to the floor as she tossed them aside in her search for some hidden treasure.

"Here it is!" she cried in triumph, holding up a book with crisp new leather binding as she hopped down from the stool. "Papa would've had a fit if he'd caught me reading it, so I had to hide it."

Ashley peered at the old-fashioned gilt lettering on the cover. "*Uncle Tom's Cabin?* I read that in English, and it was the most boring book—" She caught herself. "I mean, well, what did *you* think?" She couldn't imagine what was so terrible that Violet would have to hide it from her father.

Violet sank down on the footstool, her skirts and petticoats spread out around her like the petals of a chrysanthemum. Her face, as she clutched the book to her breast, was one of pure rapture.

"It changed my life," she said with a sigh. "I mean, when Elliot first talked about slavery, I didn't give a fig about his ideas. Free the slaves? Why, we've always had slaves at Oakehurst, I told him. Most of them—Mammy, Belle, Mince, Tucker—they're like part of the family. It just didn't seem right, the idea of casting them out to starve in the streets on account of what a few harebrained Yankees thought."

Ashley shivered in spite of the sweltering heat. What Violet was talking about—freeing the slaves—well, that's what the Civil War was fought over. In Mrs. Killington's class it had all seemed so ancient. But here she was actually *living* it.

This is weird, she thought. And getting weirder.

". . . Then Elliot gave me this book," Violet continued passionately. "I don't see how you could have thought it was boring, Le— I mean, Ashley. I cried so hard I had to wring my pillow out afterward. Honestly! Didn't you think it was sad when Little Eva died?"

Ashley had thought it was kind of sappy, but she didn't say so. "Oh, yeah, that part was really sad."

"But that wasn't the real point," Violet said. "All that stuff about slavery, and Uncle Tom. Well, I realized how naïve I'd been. No one had ever asked Mince or Tucker or Mammy if they wanted to work for us. It's like Papa always expecting me to follow his orders. And I'll bet slaves feel the same way about it. Besides, Elliot's told me—and I know it's true, because I've seen it myself—that not everyone's as nice to their slaves as we are. Elliot's right. It's just not fair!"

Ashley sat down on the bed, stunned by Violet's outburst. This was the Violet of her portrait, the firebrand of Mom's stories. The true Violet, under all those ruffles and fluttering eyelashes, was someone who really *cared*.

"You know something, Violet?" said Ashley, "I really do think you and I will be good friends."

Ashley hated to think about being marooned in this century forever, but at least she could clutch on to the small comfort of knowing she wouldn't be totally alone.

"How about this one? No, it never looked right with my hair, and yours is just as red." Violet tossed a pink gown onto the growing pile of satins and silks at the foot of her bed.

Several hours had passed since Ashley's arrival, and the talk had turned to the ball to be held at the neighboring plantation of Fairfield the following day. Violet was determined that Ashley should go, despite her protestations, and even more determined to find Ashley the right dress to wear.

Ashley went along with it all, and even tried to show some enthusiasm, but she was hoping desperately that by the time the ball took place she'd have figured out a way to return home.

Violet reached into her closet again. "Oh, Ashley, this would look perfect on you. And it would be so fitting if you wore it. It's the gown I had on the night I met Elliot."

With a lovesick sigh and a rustle of fabric, Violet pulled out a gown of brilliant emerald taffeta. The narrow bodice was outlined with strips of black lace onto which had been sewn tiny glistening beads of jet, and a net of the same black lace embroidered with jet lay over the voluminous skirt. As Violet spread it out over the bed, it shimmered and sparkled like a forest pool on a moonlit night.

Ashley fingered the froth of black lace framing the plunging neckline. "I can see why Elliot fell for you in this dress . . . but it's definitely not me. I'm not the Scarlett O'Hara type." Oops! Ashley realized too late she'd let another one of her bloopers slip out.

Violet's creamy forehead crinkled in a puzzled frown. "Scarlett O-Who?"

"She's nobody you'd know," Ashley quickly explained. "Just a girl who likes to flirt a lot."

Violet laughed. "That's practically every girl I know!"

"Except me." Ashley sank down on the bed amid the shimmering billows of fabric. "I'm hopeless when it comes to boys. If I go to this ball with you tomorrow, I'll probably just embarrass you."

Violet rushed to Ashley's side, enveloping her in another one of her rib-crushing hugs. "Mercy, don't say such things! You could never embarrass me. You're a very special person, Ashley Beaumont. I could tell that from the very start."

"You mean weird." Ashley snorted.

"Weird?"

"It means really different. Out of this world."

Oh, Violet, if you only knew how out of this world I really am, she added silently.

"But that's what makes you so special," Violet protested. "Honestly, Ash, you're not like the other girls I know. You're much more like your brother. You think for yourself, you have ideas. You're not just a silly ninny who only cares about parties and filling up your dance card."

Ashley fingered the slippery taffeta. "That sounds like 'She's got a great personality, but . . .'"

56

She appreciated what Violet was saying, but it didn't help how awkward she felt about going to this ball. Once again, she found herself praying that she wouldn't have to be put to the test, that she'd be back home in Westdale by then. But what if she weren't? She'd already been here for several hours. What if it turned into several days? Or, heaven forbid, even longer? In that case, her jitters over going to the ball would be the least of her worries . . .

Ashley sighed. And she'd thought having a crush on Len Cassinerio was complicated!

"Why, Ashley Beaumont, I don't believe what I'm hearing!" Violet stared at her, hands on hips. "It sounds to me like you don't think you're pretty enough."

"Well, that's part of it . . ."

Violet grabbed Ashley by the elbow, pulling her off the bed and steering her over to the oval-shaped floor-length mirror alongside the dresser. "You look in that mirror and tell me what you see," she ordered.

Ashley gave in to a small smile. Violet sounded a lot like Lou. But as she stared at herself in the wavy glass, her smile faded. "I see red hair. Pale skin. And eyes the color of mud."

"In that case . . ." Violet's heart-shaped face was reflected in the glass as she peered over Ashley's shoulder. Her bright red hair, done up in its twin bouquets of sausage curls, danced beside Ashley's, which hung limp and straight to her shoulders. "Then you must think I'm ugly as well."

Ashley was shocked. "You? Oh, Violet, of course I don't think that!"

"But you must admit we look alike. I have the same red hair and brown eyes and pale skin. Wouldn't it be funny if we had distant relatives in common? That's not completely unlikely, you know. Practically everyone from around here is related to one another somehow or other."

If you only knew, Ashley thought. Aloud, she said, "But you're . . ." Her voice trailed off. She didn't know quite how to put it. Violet wasn't beautiful, either. But there was something shining from within her that lit up her features like the sun on stained glass. "My moth— I mean, my brother told me you had more boys chasing after you than any other girl in the county."

Violet blushed. "That was before Elliot, of course. But that's not the point. Men can be such silly creatures, anyway. There are plenty of girls prettier than me, only the men just don't know it. Girls like Gabriella Rivers, who just sit back and expect to be admired all the time. What a man wants is a girl who admires *him*. It's funny how the more interested you act in a man, the prettier he thinks you are."

Ashley turned away from the mirror to face Violet. "I guess I never thought about it that way." Violet was a lot sharper than she'd realized.

"You can start practicing tomorrow afternoon. There'll be a big barbecue before the dance, and that's when the boys go around getting their names on the ladies' dance cards."

A sliver of panic wedged itself into Ashley's stomach. It had been bad enough sweating it out at dances in the twentieth century, hoping she'd be asked. How would this be any easier?

"It's simple," said Violet, as if she'd read Ashley's mind. "When you're introduced to a boy, lower your eyes like this—" She dropped her chin slightly, casting Ashley a slanted upward glance through her lowered lashes. "Then you find out what he's interested in, and no matter what it is, you say, 'How fascinating!' "

"How fascinating!" Ashley mimicked, Southern accent and all. Then spoiled it with a giggle.

"You see how easy it is?" Violet said. "Next thing you know, he'll ask you to dance." She whirled across the carpet in an imaginary partner's arms, her wide skirt switching gracefully in time to her dainty steps.

Dance! Ashley stared down at her own feet, peeking out from under her ruffled hem like naughty children hiding from their mother. I barely know how to do the box step without tripping over my feet, she thought. How on earth am I going to manage some fancy waltz without stepping all over my poor partner's toes?

Ashley felt as if her legs had just turned to tree trunks. "Violet, uh . . . there's this one tiny problem. I don't know how to dance."

Violet stopped whirling and simply stared at her. "Fiddlesticks! Everyone knows how to dance."

"Well, I guess I've been so busy with my compu—I mean, my schoolwork—that I never really had a chance to learn." It wasn't strictly true. She had taken lessons, along with everyone else in school, but the results had been so humiliating she didn't like to think about it. So now what she was stuck with was a head full of dance steps and two left feet that couldn't seem to execute them.

Despair rose in her, nearly overflowing into tears. What makes me think I can get back to Westdale, she wondered, when I can't even manage a simple thing like learning how to dance properly?

She was certain Violet must feel as disgusted with her as she did. This is where she gives up on me, Ashley thought nervously. She'll declare I'm hopeless and send me back to where I came from. Only I don't know how to go back. I'm stuck without Merlin. What will I tell her? What will I *do?*

But to Ashley's surprise, Violet wasn't about to give up on her. She stepped in front of Ashley, taking Ashley's right hand in her left, placing her other hand lightly against the small of Ashley's back.

Violet's amber eyes sparkled with challenge. "Well, then, Ashley Beaumont, I'd say it was about time you *did* learn!"

Chapter Six

"HOLD YOUR BREATH AND SUCK YOUR STOM-ach in," Violet commanded. "More!"

Clutching a bedpost for support, Ashley sucked her stomach in as far as it would go. *Oooof!* With this corset cinched about her middle, she felt as if she were being squeezed into an Adidas sneaker. Behind her, Violet tugged on the laces to make it even tighter.

"If I suck in any more, I won't be able to breathe!" Ashley gasped.

A mean thought occurred to her. Maybe I should give one to Alicia Sanchez on her next birthday—that would certainly put a cramp in her style!

But thinking about Alicia reminded her of Len . . . and home. It had been nearly a whole day since she'd left. And she was getting more and more antsy. She hadn't figured out a way to get home, and no one from the twentieth century had broken through the time barrier to rescue her yet. Did they even know where she was? Maybe they thought she'd been kidnapped! Mom and Dad and a whole squadron of police officers could be out looking for me at this very moment, it occurred to Ashley, but they'd be looking in all the wrong places.

Will I ever get back? she wondered miserably, the knot of homesickness still stuck in her throat, like a pill that wouldn't go down. Will I ever see Mom and Dad again? Or gossip with Lou over the phone? Or sleep in my own bed? Or stare at the back of Len's head in history?

Even boring old Mrs. Killington would be a welcome sight, she thought. And that must mean I'm *really* desperate.

This morning, when she'd awakened beneath the pink satin comforter in the guest room next to Violet's, Ashley had thought for a moment she was in her own room back in Westdale. Then reality had come crashing through the layers of fuzziness wrapped about her brain.

She was stuck in the past.

Maybe forever.

Ashley had felt as she had in swimming class when her dives ended in belly flops. Cold shock, then a horrible ache in her gut.

"It doesn't matter if you can't breathe." Violet's voice broke through her thoughts. She gave the laces another hard tug.

"Help! I'm being crushed by a python!" Ashley wheezed.

"We have to make your waist small enough, or you won't be able to fasten the buttons on your dress."

"Can't I just wear the one I had on yesterday?" Silently, Ashley blessed Brett's sister for having a larger waist than Violet's.

"Land sakes, Ash! Have you taken leave of *all* your senses?" Violet cried in exasperation. "No lady in her right mind would be caught dead wearing an afternoon dress to a ball."

"Can't I at least wear it to the barbecue?" She wouldn't be able to get a bite of anything past her Adam's apple in this thing.

"Certainly not. You'll borrow one of mine. It may be a bit short, since you're taller than I am, but at least Brett Hathaway won't be seeing you in the same dress twice in a row."

"What's Brett Hathaway got to do with it?"

Violet mercifully stopped tugging and came around to face Ashley. Wrapped in a pale blue robe, with her flame-colored hair still scrambled from sleep, she almost succeeded in making Ashley feel at home, as if this were the morning after a sleepover at one of her friends' houses.

"I saw the way he was looking at you," she said, her mouth curving up in a knowing smile. "Now, don't fib to me, Ash—you can't tell me you don't think he's handsome."

Ashley summoned up a picture of Brett Hathaway in her mind. The truth was, with everything else on her mind, she'd forgotten him until this moment. "Yes, I suppose he is."

She tried hard to hold on to the picture of Brett, but he kept floating away. In his place, she saw Len. It was strange, wasn't it? She rarely saw more than the back of Len's head, yet he filled her thoughts . . . even now, being so far away.

"There's no supposing about it," Violet said decisively. "In fact, I had my heart set on him myself once upon a time . . . way before I met Elliot. But I always got the feeling Brett preferred a more serious type of girl. Like you," she added, giving Ashley's corset a mischievous tweak.

"Who me? Serious?" Ashley crossed her eyes and stuck her tongue out at Violet.

Both girls collapsed on the bed in a storm of giggles.

There was a knock at the door.

"Come in!" Violet sang.

A plump black woman in a starched white apron, with a kerchief wrapped about her head, entered the room carrying a heavily laden tray. She set it down with a rattle of cups and plates on the table at the foot of the bed.

"Your breakfast, Miz Violet and Miz Ashley. Mammy told me to bring it up while it was still pipin' hot."

"Thank you, Mince," Violet said, lifting a cover from one of the plates to reveal a towering stack of steaming buckwheat cakes. "But Mammy doesn't really expect us to eat all this, does she?"

"Every bite." Mince folded her arms across her chest. "And I'm not s'posed to take it down till you're done."

Violet rolled her eyes at Ashley. "Mammy wants us to be so stuffed that when we get to the barbecue, we'll only peck at the food like sparrows. According to Mammy, no man worth having would be attracted to a girl with a healthy appetite. Don't ask me why. Maybe they think we'll be cheaper to feed once we're married to them," she said disdainfully.

"She shouldn't worry," Ashley said. "I couldn't swallow more than a crumb in this thing, anyhow. You go ahead, Violet. I'm not very hungry."

"Oh, no!" With both hands on Ashley's shoulders, Violet forced her down into one of the chairs. "If you think I'm eating all this by myself, you're plumb crazy." She held out a fork. "You don't know my Mammy. She'll tan both our hides if we don't do as she says."

"Shall I draw your bath while you're eatin', Miz Violet?" asked Mince.

Violet glanced down at her plate with a guilty expression. "Oh, please don't bother, Mince . . . I've already washed. You just go on ahead. We'll be fine. And I promise we'll eat every bite."

As soon as Mince was gone, Violet put her fork down and pushed her plate aside. "You see what I mean? I just can't feel right about it anymore, Mince waiting on me. I'd have dearly loved a bath, but it would've taken her an hour to prepare it! All those kettles of hot water carried upstairs. Why should she have to do what I'm perfectly capable of doing myself?"

Ashley was mystified. Kettles of hot water? Was the bathtub faucet broken or something?

Then it struck her. Oh, yeah. Indoor plumbing hasn't been invented yet. Remember how Violet laughed when you asked her what that pot under the bed was for?

She forced her mind back to what Violet was saying. "I'd feel the same way myself," Ashley replied. "Slavery *is* wrong."

Ashley thought about the experiment her science teacher, Mr. Macklin, had conducted the year before last. He divided the class into two groups, the brown eyes versus the blue and green eyes. The brown eyes had to act as slaves for the blue and green eyes the first day, and vice versa the second day. Ashley remembered thinking what a dumb experiment it was at first—Mr. Macklin was always coming up with these crazy humanistic assignments that had very little to do with science.

But it turned out to be one of the most jolting experiences Ashley had ever had. She would never forget the anger and resentment she'd felt, having someone boss her around and being powerless to fight back.

When her own turn came around to do the bossing, she'd simply refused. No one has the right to turn someone else into a slave, she'd told Mr. Macklin. He'd merely grinned, his blue eyes crinkling with satisfaction behind his John Denver glasses.

She'd gotten an A on the assignment.

It was even more remarkable, Ashley thought, for someone like Violet, who had grown up around slaves, to feel such compassion and indignation. Her respect for Violet soared up a few more notches.

"I just wish Mammy would show some sympathy for me," moaned Violet. "However am I going to eat all this?"

Ashley moaned in sympathy, spearing a bite of one of the buckwheat cakes with her fork. She didn't fear a scolding from Mammy as Violet did, but it was the least she could do to help Violet after all the kindness Violet had shown her.

Besides, she thought, if I burst out of this corset like the Goodyear blimp, then maybe I won't have to go to the ball after all.

Violet finished buttoning the last of the tiny buttons that held Ashley's dress together in back. "There." She clapped her hands in delight. "You look absolutely divine, Ashley. If Brett Hathaway doesn't hurry, you'll have every last dance on your card taken before he can blink an eye."

Ashley stood back to look at herself in the wavy glass of the oval mirror. What an incredible transformation! It was like one of those Before and After makeovers you saw in magazines.

"Wow, I've got curves!" she cried. At least there was some consolation for being squeezed into this torture-chamber device they called a corset.

She was even beginning to get used to seeing herself in dresses that made her look like a wedding cake. This one that Violet had lent her was even prettier than the one she'd had on the day before. It was a sky blue cotton gown, with tiny flowers embroidered down the bodice. As Violet had predicted, it was a little short, since she was at least three inches taller than Violet, but with all the ruffles cascading from the hem, it was hardly noticeable. Anyway, she was too busy staring at the reflection of her chest to notice what was going on down by her ankles.

I don't look like an ironing board! she observed with a small shock of delight. Now I can see why Violet made me wear that ruffled camisole underneath the dress. All those little rows of ruffles and tucks sewn across the front really have a purpose. And it sure beats those rolled-up socks I used to stuff in my bra when I was home alone, just to see what it would look like.

In addition to the camisole, she was wearing a slip that could have served as a parachute under her skirt. It was like the one she'd worn yesterday—a wide hoop sewn into the hem, with three smaller hoops above it, the smallest one just below her waist. But this petticoat's hoops were much wider.

Talk about circus tents! I could probably hide an elephant under here. How am I ever going to manage a step without crashing into something?

"Maybe if I climbed out the window, I could just float down," Ashley said, holding her skirt out like a parachute.

"Not after all those hotcakes you ate." Violet giggled. "*You* would be as flat as one after you fell. And speaking of flat"—she lifted a limp strand of Ashley's hair—"we simply *must* do something about this hair of yours."

"There's not much you can do, I'm afraid," Ashley said, tucking it behind her ears. "It's too short to put up on my head, and it never holds a curl for longer than five minutes."

"Fiddlesticks! You'll wear one of my hairpieces, that's all. Lucky for you, the color will match." Violet began toying with Ashley's hair. "What I don't understand is how your hair ever ended up that way in the first place? I don't mean to be insulting, Ash, but I've simply never seen the likes of it."

Ashley sighed. "It's a long story, Violet. Someday I'll tell you all about it."

"Oh, I think I understand . . . another one of your Yankee customs?" In the mirror, Ashley saw Violet arch one brow in a look that said she thought that excuse was wearing pretty thin.

Violet is no dummy, Ashley thought. She knows I'm hiding something. She's just too polite to ask what it is. How I wish I could tell her! But how can I expect her to believe who I am and where I'm really from? Westdale and the world I know would seem as way-out as Mars to Violet. Ashley sighed deeply, homesickness squeezing her as tightly as her corset.

"Don't fret, I promise you'll love it when I'm finished," Violet said, mistaking the source of her down mood, as she continued to comb and pin Ashley's hair.

Ashley forced a little smile for Violet's sake. "Oh, I'm sure I will."

I only wish I could be as sure about getting home, she thought, worry nibbling at her insides with tiny sharp teeth. When Mom and Dad run out of obvious places to look for me, how will they ever guess where I've gone? Will Lou remember enough of what I've told her about my time-traveling experiment to help them? Or is it up to me to find my own way home?

Once again, Ashley pondered the question of Violet and

66

Elliot. But even if their marriage—or lack of it—was at the root of her problems, she didn't have the foggiest idea what to do about it.

Face it, she told herself. At this very moment, there isn't a thing you can do. Except wait and see what happens.

"There!" Violet's voice broke into her thoughts. "All done." With Violet's hairpiece pinned atop her head, and her own embarrassing hair tucked underneath, Ashley's makeover was complete.

She tried hard to turn her thoughts to the here and now. Worrying isn't going to get you home, she reminded herself. And if you don't start concentrating on what's going on around you, you'll never get through this ball without making a fool of yourself.

Seated before the dressing table, she peered at herself from all angles in the silver hand mirror Violet handed her. Is it me? Ashley wondered, her worries momentarily melting away in the face of her startling transformation.

A shiver of delight rippled through her, and she rubbed her bare arms to smooth out the goosebumps. I never would have believed it, but it's true—what Lou and Violet have been trying to tell me—I really *am* pretty.

"Violet, you ought to open a beauty salon," Ashley blurted out.

"Hhmmm?" Violet mumbled through a mouthful of hairpins.

"Never mind. I'm just acting weird again." Would she ever learn to keep track of which century she was in?

Suddenly unable to keep still any longer, Ashley jumped up from her chair. Her heart was fluttering beneath her tight corset like a caged bird. In a few more minutes they would be leaving for Fairfield. Lots of people would be there. Could she manage to fool them all? Would her stomach stop doing flip-flops long enough for her to pull off the Scarlett O'Hara act Violet had so carefully instructed her in?

"Just keep your eye on me, and you'll do just fine," Violet reminded her once again as they were making their way along the front corridor to join Papa Oakes outside, where the carriage awaited. She lifted her skirt above her knees to show Ashley how she stood slightly pigeon-toed. "See how my skirt sways when I walk with my toes pointed in? It's a little trick I learned from my cousin Eulalie. It simply drives the boys to distraction!"

But Ashley's problem was just the opposite. She hadn't figured out yet how to keep her skirts from *not* moving all over the place. She carefully maneuvered her way around the furniture.

"I feel like a float in the Rose Bowl Parade," Ashley muttered. "Oops!" Her immense skirt went flying against a graceful end table and sent it teetering.

There was a loud crash, and she looked down in horror at the porcelain figurine in pieces on the marble floor. She wanted to cry, but she couldn't even manage that with her corset laced so tightly.

I'll never get the hang of this, Ashley thought. Never. Tears of frustration welled up in her eyes. I may look the part, but I'm still a walking disaster.

Violet daintily sidestepped the broken pieces on the floor. "Rose bowl? Mercy, Ash, that was a china shepherdess you broke. But never mind, we've got to hurry. Papa will be impatient." She patted Ashley's shoulder, adding mischievously, "Just be careful you don't go breaking poor Brett Hathaway's heart the same way!"

Ashley looked down at Violet, so taken aback she nearly forgot about the broken figurine. Me, break someone's heart? Violet doesn't know what she's talking about! She thinks I'm like *her,* so irresistible boys will just fall all over themselves to be near me.

If only that were true—at least as far as Len was concerned!

Nevertheless, Violet's confidence in her lifted Ashley's spirits somewhat. She managed to sail down the front steps toward the waiting carriage without further mishap, except for catching her hem briefly on a rose thorn.

Now for the real test—meeting all of Violet's friends and

neighbors. Would she be able to fool them into accepting her as she had Violet and Brett? Or would they see right through her? Ashley wanted to run away and hide, but there was no turning back now. She would just have to try her hardest and hope for the best.

A fact gleaned from one of Mrs. Killington's lectures leaped up to taunt her now. She remembered hearing how sometimes strangers were tarred and feathered before being run out of town. What a horrible thought! That couldn't happen to me, could it? she wondered in panic, feeling herself break out in an icy sweat.

As she stepped up into the carriage and met Papa Oakes's disapproving gaze, Ashley shuddered. At that moment she could easily imagine what it would feel like to be dipped in hot tar and rolled in feathers.

Chapter Seven

"EVERYBODY . . . I WANT Y'ALL TO MEET MY good friend Ashley Beaumont!" Violet sang out to the crowd gathered on the lush green lawn at Fairfield.

Ashley stared out at the sea of ruffles and bobbing parasols, waistcoats and top hats. A familiar bubble of panic wiggled up her throat. She was certain every one of them could read her mind and knew exactly what she was thinking.

Help! she cried silently. I can't do this. They're going to know I'm a fake the minute I open my mouth. They probably know it already.

But at the same time, she felt irresistibly drawn to the scene before her. It was like some kind of paradise. Girls in their wedding-cake dresses flirted with handsome young men. Little children played on the emerald grass beneath a magnolia tree bursting with creamy white blossoms that filled the air with a lemony scent.

There were no planes roaring overhead. No car fumes. No racket of radios. Just the soft murmur of voices in the drowsy spring air, and the sweet smell of magnolias.

Ashley felt her panic ebb. It was all so beautiful. Maybe she could never really be a part of it, but she could pretend for a little while, couldn't she?

Something her friend Kiki Wykowski once said came to mind: "When you can't be yourself, just pick a part and pretend you're an actress."

Easy for Kiki. She really was an actress. Probably the

best one O. Henry High had ever seen. But it made sense. All I have to do is pretend I'm Scarlett O'Hara, Ashley thought.

Violet led her over to a patch of shade beneath a huge oak tree. Stretched below it was a long table spread with more food than Ashley had ever seen in one place in her entire life. Platters of roasted meat, corn on the cob, golden biscuits, vast steaming bowls of potatoes and vegetables, sliced watermelons, and every kind of pie imaginable. It almost made Ashley wish she were hungry.

But she promptly forgot her appetite as several young men and women crowded about.

"Ah'm pleased to make your acquaintance, Miss Beaumont!" A boy with curly blond hair bowed so low before her that Ashley was afraid he'd bump his nose on his kneecap. "Ah'm Sandy DuBois."

"My, what an absolutely divine dress!" gushed a plump girl who was so tightly squeezed into her own cranberry-colored dress that she looked pop-eyed.

"I declare, Violet," said a girl with sparkling green eyes, "she could be your very own sister with that hair of hers. Are you sure you haven't been hiding her over at Oakehurst all these years?"

Violet let loose a tinkling laugh. "Gracious, Lavinia, wouldn't *you* . . . if you had a sister as pretty as Ashley? But she's far too sweet to be jealous of. I sincerely wish she *were* my sister!"

Ashley wanted to hug Violet on the spot, but she was afraid she'd pop a few buttons if she tried. She wished she and Violet could be sisters, too. It was hard to keep remembering that Violet was really her great-great-grandmother.

She caught Violet's eye, and they smiled at one another. Then Violet's gaze wandered, and her smile faded. As she stared at something—or someone—beyond Ashley, her face grew pale.

"Forgive me for rushing off, Ash," she whispered hurriedly, "but I see someone I don't wish to talk to . . ."

71

Ashley watched as Violet darted away, her dress a splash of bright blue against the velvety green of the lawn as she headed toward the veranda. A heavyset man, his square jaw framed by a dense black beard, set off in pursuit, but she disappeared behind a tall white pillar before he could reach her.

Who is he? Ashley wondered. And why is Violet trying to avoid him? It looks like I'm not the only one with secrets around here!

Before she could take off after Violet herself, Ashley heard a deep voice ask, "May I get you something cool to drink, Miss Beaumont?"

It was the boy with the blond curls who had spoken to her before. Why is he staring at me like that? Ashley wondered nervously. Heat began creeping up into her cheeks.

Then she remembered what she was supposed to do. Act like Scarlett O'Hara. Now that Violet had shown her all the tricks, she certainly knew the part well enough.

Ashley opened the fan that dangled from a silken cord tied to her wrist. Lowering her gaze, she fluttered the fan in front of her face the way Violet had shown her.

"How did you guess?" she cooed in her best Scarlett imitation. "I was just standing here thinking I would probably faint if I didn't get something cool to drink."

Wow! Did I really say that? Ashley wondered. I must have picked up more from Mom than I ever realized. That sounded exactly like something she would have said.

And look . . . it's working. He's not laughing at me. Amazing!

Flashing her a gallant grin, he dashed over to the refreshment table, returning a few seconds later with a tall dripping glass. What was his name? Oh, yes. Sandy something.

Ashley accepted the glass, remembering to flutter her eyelashes as she did so. "Sandy. Is that just short for your real name, or do they call you Sandy because your hair is that color?"

See, that wasn't so hard, she congratulated herself. That was probably the dumbest thing you've ever said to a boy, but he's acting as if he thinks you're the hottest thing in petticoats.

Hey, this is actually kind of fun!

"My grandfather's name was Sanderson," he said shyly. "He was one of the first settlers in these parts."

What next? Ashley struggled to think of a response. Then she remembered what Violet had told her.

"How fascinating!" she cried. She couldn't think what was supposed to be so fascinating about what he'd said. But it didn't seem to matter. Sandy was blushing with delight at her interest.

He took her elbow lightly, steering her toward the path that wound through the rose garden, where several other couples were strolling. "Why, yes, it is. He built our plantation back in—"

Sandy was interrupted as another boy—stocky and dark-haired, wearing a crimson waistcoat—sauntered across their path.

"That's a fine kettle of fish for you!" cried the dark-haired stranger. "You've scarcely been introduced, and Sandy is stealing away with you. At least allow me to put my name down for a waltz, Miss Beaumont."

Ashley was so flustered she forgot she was supposed to be Scarlett O'Hara and nearly plunged straight into a rosebush. But she pulled back just in time.

"Waltz? Uh, sure— I mean, why, certainly." She held out the dance card, which dangled from a cord around her wrist alongside her fan.

No sooner had the dark-haired boy filled in his name than the card was snatched from his grasp by Sandy, who hastily scribbled his name in four of the blanks.

Ashley's mind whirled with all the attention she was getting. It didn't seem possible. Me, she thought. They want *me*. Whatever I said—or did—it worked. Now if only I could find a way to bottle it and take it back to the twentieth century with me . . .

"Don't forget, the first waltz is mine," said a familiar voice behind her.

Ashley whirled to find Brett Hathaway smiling at her, his hat pushed back from his forehead at a rakish angle. He was even taller than she'd remembered. He wore a plum-colored waistcoat and a dark blue cravat that matched the color of his eyes. His smooth glossy dark hair gleamed in the sunlight.

He plucked a tiny pink tea rose from the bush she'd nearly tumbled into and handed it to her. As their fingers brushed, Ashley felt an odd tingle. Scarlett O'Hara, meet Rhett Butler, she thought.

But you're not really Scarlett, she reminded herself. You're only pretending to be. So just don't get too carried away with the part.

"You seem a mite sad, Miss Beaumont. Don't tell me you're homesick already?" Brett Hathaway's hand pressed firmly against Ashley's back as he guided her onto the dance floor.

Ashley pulled her gaze from the magical scene before her—a kaleidoscope of bright silks and satins twirling across the polished floorboards, the twinkle of waistcoat buttons reflecting the glow of a hundred candles. Violin music swirled about her like a current, punctuated by bursts of high girlish laughter and the tinkle of crystal.

She concentrated on Brett's face, hovering near hers with an expression of concern. "Uh . . . yes, I guess I was thinking about home."

This is all so beautiful, she thought. But it could never be home. I feel like Dorothy, stuck in the Emerald City, homesick for Kansas.

She tried to imagine what was going on in Westdale right now. Mom and Dad must be worried sick. They would have notified the police by now, and probably Andy, too.

The Conn-Tech picnic would have been canceled, no doubt, and everyone would know what had happened—people around town, her friends, the kids at school—everyone. Including Len Cassinerio.

The thought of Len caused her heart to beat faster. Would

he miss her? Now that she was gone, would he realize she'd meant more to him than just a warm body behind him in history? Ashley allowed herself a tiny flicker of satisfaction at the idea that Len might be among those searching for her at this very moment, frantic with worry.

But her satisfaction was short-lived. They wouldn't find her in any of the usual places, she realized, coming to earth with a crash of despair. Because I won't exist for another hundred years. If at all.

How long would it take before they figured out where she'd gone? Or would they ever? After all, it wasn't every day people got lost in the past. It would take a real stretch of her parents' imagination for them to figure out what had happened to her. And even if they did eventually, would they be able to figure out they had to turn off Merlin to get her back? Even Dad's top Conn-Tech engineers might not be able to unravel the secrets of her fractal program. Her stomach rolled over at the thought.

"Miss Beaumont?" Brett's smooth drawl interrupted her thoughts, abruptly pulling her back from the brink of panic.

Ashley blinked, bringing him back into focus. "I'm sorry. I guess I'm not very good company."

He smiled, his teeth a flash of white against his swarthy face. "I wouldn't go so far as to say that. In fact, if you must know, I find your company most charming." He caught her about the waist, and swung her into the midst of the waltzing couples.

Before she knew what was happening, Ashley found herself waltzing in time with the beat, her feet gliding over the floor alongside Brett's, twirling, swooping . . .

Wow, I'm really dancing! she thought, images of home dimming as the music took over. Violet's lessons really worked! I'm—

Wait a minute! I can't dance. I'm a hopeless klutz.

Panic turned her limbs to wood. Suddenly, she felt like a marionette jerking out of control, getting tangled up in its strings. It didn't help either that she wasn't used to these satin shoes of Violet's, which were a little tight on Ashley, even though Violet had big feet for someone so dainty. Her heel caught in the lace flounce at her hem, and she heard a small ripping sound. *Oops!* She craned to inspect the damage, grateful to see that it was minor. But before she could breathe a sigh of relief, she nearly lost her balance. She managed to regain it, but ended up stamping on Brett's foot, instead. He stumbled, wincing in pain.

Gasping for breath, her cheeks flushed with heat, Ashley clung to him for support. "Oh, Brett, it's no use! I can't dance. I can barely walk without tripping over myself." She became aware that people were staring at them, and her face grew even hotter. She lowered her voice, "Look, this isn't fair to you. Why don't I just let you off the hook?"

"Off the hook?" He stared at her, looking perplexed.

"It means you don't have to dance with me anymore. I'm officially releasing you from your obligation."

Brett laughed. "You mean you're going to be a coward about it."

"Coward?" She stared at him, confused. Klutz, yes. But coward? After all, she'd only be doing him a favor!

"Indeed, Miss Beaumont. And frankly, I'm surprised. For a girl who dares to wear pants and ride a horse like a man, I'd say you're behaving like a sissy. You're quitting before you've given yourself a fair chance."

Ashley was so stunned, she didn't know what to say. "You mean . . . you still *want* to dance with me?"

Brett didn't answer. He merely smiled, and took her lightly in his arms once again. In his plum-colored waistcoat with its gold buttons, he reminded Ashley of Prince Charming.

"We'll go more slowly this time," he murmured, easing into the first step. "And you must try not to think so hard. Just feel the music . . . Yes, that's it. You see, Miss Beaumont, you're a better dancer than you realized."

Brett's confidence was infectious. Soon Ashley began to feel it, too. And once she stopped being so nervous, her arms and legs miraculously began cooperating with the rest of her.

Maybe Lou was right, she thought. I was so busy trying not to be clumsy, I had myself all tied into knots. How had Lou put it? Just like when someone tells you not to think about elephants, and all you can think about is elephants.

The loud voices of two men rose above the lilting music, interrupting Ashley's thoughts.

"I say we're wasting time. We ought to take up arms against those Yankees before another sun has set!" the first man shouted.

"I'm not saying I'm against the notion, but confound it, Gerald, don't you think you're being rash about this whole thing?" The second man spoke in a steady voice. "I hear tell that scoundrel Abraham Lincoln has whole armies mobilized, and factories, and warehouses . . . and, well, what have we got but cotton and slaves?"

Ashley looked up at Brett, alarmed. "What are those men arguing about?"

Brett's smile faded, and his blue eyes seemed to darken. "What else does anyone argue about these days? War. They say it's going to be declared any day now."

Holy moly! He means the Civil War. It's so incredible. Here I am, Ashley Calhoun from twentieth-century Westdale, Connecticut, about to experience the Civil War firsthand! That must have been why the date 1861 rang a bell back when I was programming Merlin.

Ashley wished now she'd paid more attention in Mrs. Killington's class. But it had all seemed so ancient and boring then. Now panic swept through her. Real people—people she knew—could be killed.

"Will you fight when— I mean, if it's declared?" she asked Brett nervously.

He stared deep into her eyes. "I know what you must be thinking, Miss Beaumont. But this doesn't change my feelings toward you. And I . . . I hope we can remain friends, regardless of our differing views."

Ashley was momentarily distracted by the sight of Violet, looking stiff and gloomy as she danced past in the

77

arms of the black-bearded man she'd been running away from earlier. Apparently, he'd managed to trap her after all, and she didn't look too happy about it.

As soon as we're alone, I'll coax the whole story out of her, Ashley told herself.

Then she lost sight of Violet. She became aware that she and Brett had drifted very close to the French windows that stood open, leading onto the veranda. The magnolia-scented breeze floating in felt deliciously cool against her flushed cheeks.

The violins stopped playing, and Brett led her onto the deserted veranda. In the moonlight, the grass and trees beyond the stone balustrade gleamed silver, and the creamy waxlike blossoms covering the enormous old magnolia tree seemed to float ghostlike in the stillness.

"On a night like this, it doesn't seem possible that we'll be fighting a war soon," Brett said softly in the darkness. "But they say it won't last more than a day. A week at the very most."

"Oh, Brett." Ashley's voice caught. She'd learned enough in Mrs. Killington's class to know how wrong Brett was. "It won't be over in a week. It'll go on for years. Thousands of people will die. And whole cities will be destroyed. And—"

She stopped, aware that Brett was staring at her in that odd way.

"You are the darndest girl I've ever met. Where in tarnation did you get such an absurd idea?"

"From history books!" Ashley blurted.

"Ancient history, no doubt. The Greeks and the Romans. Now"—he leaned close, placing a warm hand against her cheek—"let's have no more talk about war. I don't want anything to come between us."

Ashley felt herself go all tingly. His hand was so warm against her cheek. His eyes dark and liquid as they gazed into hers.

Brett's words echoed in her mind. *I don't want anything to come between us.*

When did we become *us?* she wondered.

Is Brett falling in love with me? Or—oh my gosh, can it be?—am I falling in love with him?

Ashley's head spun. It was like something out of *Gone with the Wind*. The soft spring air. The scent of magnolias. The music drifting out onto the veranda. She was Scarlett, and Rhett Butler was about to kiss her. She shut her eyes. He was so close she could feel his breath against her cheek . . .

"Oh, Rhett . . ." she murmured.

"Rhett?" He chuckled softly. "I like it. I've never had a nickname before."

Ashley's eyes flew open. Had she really said that? Oh, what on earth had she been thinking?

A cold shower of reality woke Ashley from her daydreams. You're not Scarlett O'Hara, she told herself. You're Ashley Calhoun from Westdale, Connecticut. And don't you forget it.

Sure it was beautiful here, and so romantic with Brett holding her close, but she could never really belong. It was almost as if the mansions and magnolia trees were part of an elaborate movie set, and Brett was her leading man.

A wave of claustrophobia swept over her. Under this tightly laced corset, and all these layers of clothing, I'm a prisoner, she thought, panic dropping like a cold stone into the pit of her stomach. A prisoner of another time. And the American Civil War is about to begin.

Chapter Eight

"OH, ASH, I'M SO MISERABLE I COULD JUST *DIE!*"
Violet collapsed into Ashley's arms as the carriage jolted
over the bumpy dirt road to Oakehurst.

To Ashley's relief, Papa Oakes had sent them ahead
without him when the ball was over. He had gotten in-
volved in a heated discussion of war with some of the other
men as they were getting ready to leave, and had decided
to stay on a while longer at Fairfield.

Ashley stroked Violet's curls. Poor Violet! What could
have upset her so? Ashley felt a twinge of guilt. Had she
been so wrapped up in her own anxiety these past two days
that she'd ignored the warning signs leading up to this flood
of misery?

Violet always acts so lighthearted, Ashley reflected. As
if her life were nothing more than an endless round of
barbecues and balls, and her biggest problem choosing
which dress to wear to what occasion. But I know she's
much deeper and more sensitive than that. Look how in-
dignant she feels about slavery, for instance. And how she's
helped me see myself in a better light. And what about
Elliot? When she speaks of him, I can see the love shining
from her eyes. He's not just another passing flirtation as
far as Violet's concerned. She's willing to risk throwing
aside everything for him—her family, her whole Southern
tradition, all the other boyfriends she could have.

Suddenly it struck Ashley. The reason Violet was so
upset. How could she have been so blind?

"Is it Elliot?" she asked Violet gently. "Oh, Violet, I didn't think . . . But of course, you must miss him so much . . ."

Violet fumbled with the drawstring of the little purse that dangled from her wrist and withdrew a lacy handkerchief. She looked up at Ashley, dabbing at her eyes. "I wish with all my heart Elliot were here now," she said. "Then maybe Mr. Calvert wouldn't have taken such a fancy to me."

"Mr. Calvert?" Ashley was puzzled for an instant, then she recalled the black-bearded man she'd seen Violet with at the ball. "Is he the one you were dancing with?"

Violet nodded, her chin trembling and her tears threatening to overflow once again.

"Well, I've seen worse-looking guys," Ashley kidded, as much to lighten her own mood as Violet's. "At least he didn't have warts, or a hunchback, or—"

"It's worse." Violet moaned. "He wants to marry me!"

Ashley sat back, stunned. Marriage? He'd seemed so *old* . . . at least thirty. And Violet was only sixteen.

Still, Violet was getting herself all worked up over nothing. "It's not the end of the world," Ashley reassured her. "Can't you just tell him no?"

Violet stared down at her hands, folded tightly in her lap, and gave a long shuddering sigh. "It's not that simple, I'm afraid. Wade Calvert won't take no for an answer. He's determined to marry me, even though he knows I don't love him."

Ashley was mystified. "But that doesn't mean you *have* to, does it?"

"Papa will see it differently. Mr. Calvert's plantation is the richest in the county. And he's been alone since his wife died a year ago. Some say it was the only way she could get away from him . . ." Violet shuddered, letting the sentence trail.

"I still don't see why you should marry him just because he's rich," Ashley protested.

Violet looked up sharply. "Oh, Ash, *I* don't give a fig for his money, but Papa does. And Wade Calvert is a highly influential man in this county, too. If he asks Papa for my hand, then Papa's sure to say yes.''

Ashley jerked upright so suddenly that a jolt of the wheels nearly sent her sprawling to the floor of the carriage.

"But you can't. You've got to marry Elliot!"

If you don't, she added silently, then my whole branch of the family tree will get chopped off, which means *I'll* never get born!

Ashley's mind spun with confusion and near-hysterical panic. Was Violet's marriage to Elliot the key to her getting back after all? In which case, she realized, if Violet doesn't marry Elliot, if she marries Mr. Calvert instead, then I'll never be able to get back. Because I won't exist!

What will happen to me? she wondered, biting against the inside of her cheek to keep from crying. Will I go up in a puff of smoke, or simply fade into nothingness? The thought made her feel sick and shivery, as if she were coming down with the flu.

"You've just *got* to marry Elliot!" she repeated desperately.

"You don't know Papa," Violet said in a wobbly voice. "He's as stubborn as a mule. Nothing ever changes his mind once he's made it up. I tried to tell him I loved Elliot, but he wouldn't hear of it. Mercy, he nearly brought the roof down with all his shouting! In fact, he very nearly canceled your visit simply on account of your being Elliot's sister!'' she added, then blushed with embarrassment.

I wish he *had* canceled it, Ashley reflected miserably. Then I'd be back home where I should be. Then she realized with a sharp pang that she couldn't go back now, even if she were able to. Violet needed her to help. Her life would be ruined forever if she married Mr. Calvert.

Not to mention what might happen to mine, Ashley added silently.

It didn't make Ashley feel any better to know she might have accidentally caused the whole thing, either. It only made her feel twice as responsible. If her time jump had somehow stirred up the wrong ions in the atmosphere or something, then it was up to her to try and straighten them out.

"Maybe Mr. Calvert won't ask your father for your hand," she offered weakly.

"I've been hoping the same thing. But Mr. Calvert says he's tired of waiting around. He's been calling on me for months. But honestly, Ash, I've never given him one speck of encouragement. In fact, half the times he's called, I've pretended I was too indisposed to come down and meet him. I can't imagine why he would even *want* to marry me!"

"Maybe he thinks you're playing hard to get."

"I even told him I loved Elliot . . . but he didn't care. He sneered. He called Elliot a—a . . . yellow-bellied Yankee. Oh, how I hate him! If Papa forces me to marry him, I—I'll just *die!*"

Ashley hugged Violet. "You won't have to marry Mr. Calvert," she said more forcefully than she felt. "Don't worry, Violet, I'll help you find a way out."

"How?" wailed Violet.

"I don't know." Ashley desperately wished she could offer Violet more reassurance. But the truth was, she was plenty worried herself. "Somehow."

Back at Oakehurst, in the room adjoining Violet's, Ashley lay in the enormous four-poster bed, staring up at the ceiling. She was exhausted, but sleep just wouldn't come.

Visions of the past and present flashed across her mind like some crazy slide show. And the slides kept getting mixed up. She saw her father at the barbecue. He was standing before the roasting pit in his chef's apron that said "Love and Quiches," waving at the smoke with a long-handled spatula. Ashley's eyes prickled with tears.

She saw Violet in her froth of skirts, stepping daintily from the school bus in front of O. Henry High.

Forward and back. Images jerked out of sequence, until she felt like a Ping-Pong ball bouncing between two worlds, two centuries.

Ashley saw herself at the ball, whirling across the dance floor in Brett's arms. Except when she looked at his face, he wasn't Brett anymore. It was Len who held her in his arms, gazing down at her with those sleepy Rambo eyes as he waltzed her around . . . and around . . . and around . . .

"Yo, Ashley, I really missed you. Mrs. K.'s class hasn't been the same since you left . . ."

A tear trickled down Ashley's temple into her hair. Oh, Len! Will I ever see you again? Will I see any of you? Len, right now I would give a million dollars even to see Mrs. Killington again. Because that would mean I was back where I belonged, back in the good old 1980's.

It's not that I don't like it here, she continued her imaginary conversation with Len. There are parts of it that are really beautiful and exciting. The best part is Violet. She's becoming like a sister to me. And, wow, can you believe I actually found a way to travel back in time? It's awesome!

But, oh, Len, I miss Westdale so much. My family and all my friends . . . and you, of course. This is even worse than that terminal case of homesickness I had my first summer away at Camp Weewuk. Because I don't know if I'll ever be able to go home.

And I would give anything to be there, even if . . . if it meant tripping on my way into class every single day for the rest of the year.

I feel like E.T., trying to find a way to phone home. But I can't even do that. There's no way to make a long-distance call between here and the future.

If only I could confide in Violet! She might believe me, now that we've become friends. On the other hand, since she already thinks I'm strange, this might just convince her I'm a complete nut case.

Besides, Violet has troubles of her own. And how! If her father forces her to marry Wade Calvert, she'll lose everything she ever cared about—Oakehurst, Elliot . . .

. . . and me!

84

Ashley sat straight up in bed. I've *got* to find some way of preventing it. If only Elliot were here! Maybe he could somehow convince Papa Oakes . . .

But no, *that* wouldn't work. Because if Elliot were here, then everyone would know I wasn't really Leonore Beaumont.

Around her, the room began to spin slowly, as if she were on a carousel. Ashley lay back down and closed her eyes. No. The room wasn't really spinning. Her head was.

She pictured her brain as a circuit board hooked up to a giant computer. Green lights flashed on the control panel. A digital timer was spinning backward. The numbers moving faster and faster . . .

Ashley fell asleep, dreaming of Violet in her wedding gown at the altar . . . with Merlin at her side.

The following morning, Ashley was awakened early by Violet, who announced that they were going horseback riding. It was the only thing that could calm her nerves when she was upset like this, she told Ashley. Violet didn't have to add that she'd lain awake half the night, imagining the worst as far as Mr. Calvert was concerned. Her puffy, red-rimmed eyes told the whole story.

Ashley had done more than her share of tossing and turning, too. Yes, she thought, a day out in the country air might be what we both need in order to clear our heads and start thinking of a way out of this mess.

Shivering in the damp gray dawn, Ashley quickly washed herself, using the china basin and pitcher on the marble washstand. Then she dressed in the chocolate brown velvet riding habit Violet had tossed through the door. The jacket was a little tight, since she'd purposely left the laces on her corset loose, but the skirt fit okay. It wasn't nearly as full as the skirt on yesterday's ballgown, since it was made for riding, and thank goodness she didn't have to wear all those bothersome petticoats. Nonetheless, she would have given anything right now for an old pair of jeans and a comfortable sweatshirt.

I wish I'd known I was going to be stuck here this long, Ashley thought as she stood before the mirror, straightening her cap with its long ostrich feather that curled down to tickle her between the shoulder blades. I would have packed a suitcase.

She compiled a mental list of the things her suitcase would contain. Jeans. O. Henry High sweatshirt. Reebok running shoes. Sony Walkman and new Tina Turner tape. Toothbrush. Lipstick. Antiperspirant. And . . . oh, yes, Polaroid camera.

Just think how people would flip out if I ever showed them a photo album of *this* trip!

For a moment, Ashley indulged in the bizarre fantasy. She imagined herself sitting cross-legged on her bed back home, showing Lou snapshots of Oakehurst and the people she'd met. Would Lou think Brett Hathaway was cute? As cute as Len? A giggle escaped her lips at the idea of comparing two boys who had been born a century apart. But the giggle quickly turned to a frown of worry. Would she ever see Lou or Len again? She'd been gone for almost two days. Lou would be frantic.

Or would she?

Ashley felt as if the air had suddenly turned ice-cold. If I never got born, my friends wouldn't even know who I was, much less worry about me. The name Ashley Calhoun wouldn't mean a thing to them.

Ashley rubbed her arms, which prickled with goosebumps. And to think she'd worried about making an A-1 klutz out of herself in front of Len. At least he'd known she existed!

She let out a deep sigh. If only I'd hadn't been so eager to leap back into the past. If only I'd done more research and maybe a few more experiments. Then maybe I wouldn't have created such a mess. But isn't this just typical? I mean, when have I ever glided smoothly into *anything?* I'm always stumbling, or dropping something, so why should this have been any different?

"Need any help?" Violet poked her head into the room.

A teasing smile momentarily softened the lines of misery in her face. "I declare, I could've gone clear to Charleston and back in the time it's taken you to get dressed."

Ashley was startled to realize how long she'd been daydreaming. "Uh . . . sorry, Violet. I guess I'm just one of those people whose batteries need a jump start in the morning."

Violet shot her a puzzled look. "Batteries? What in heaven's name are you talking about, Ash?"

Ashley felt like kicking herself. "Oh, never mind. It would take forever to explain, and I've already wasted enough time as it is. C'mon, let's get going."

Violet didn't argue. From her troubled expression it was plain she had too many worries of her own at the moment to let her curiosity about Ashley's strange behavior run away with her.

Ashley crossed the room to link arms with Violet. "A nice ride will do us both good." Together, they went down the staircase and stepped out into the brisk early morning air.

The stable was a long, low building as big as an ordinary-sized house. The instant Ashley walked inside, she was surrounded by the pungent smell of horses, hay, and oiled leather. It reminded her of all those summers she'd taken riding lessons at camp. Horseback was one of the few sports she was good at—maybe because horses were a lot less apt to stumble than she was.

"Can you saddle a horse by yourself?" asked Violet. "I hate to wake Tucker up this early. Cold mornings are bad for his arthritis."

"Sure thing." Ashley didn't tell her that she'd always saddled her own horse without help from any slaves.

Violet disappeared down the row of stalls, returning a few minutes later leading two bridled horses—a beautiful chestnut mare with gentle brown eyes, and a nervous-looking black gelding.

"You take Bonnet," she said, handing Ashley the mare's reins. "She won't give you any trouble. And I'll take Lafayette. He's a devil, but it'll be good practice for standing up to Papa if I ever get the nerve.''

Violet hoisted a saddle from its peg in the tack room. Old polished leather gleamed like satin in the gray morning light. But Ashley had never before seen a saddle like this one. It was strangely shaped, and one side had no stirrup.

"Uh . . . Violet. I think there's something wrong with this saddle," she pointed out.

Violet shot her an amused glance. "Oh, Ash, there's nothing wrong with it. Haven't you ever seen a ladies' sidesaddle before? I thought you said you'd ridden before.''

"Not sidesaddle. I'd probably fall off if I sat on that thing." Ashley remembered now that sidesaddles were customary for ladies to ride during this time.

Ashley replaced the saddle Violet had chosen, choosing one of the men's saddles instead. "A lot of my weird Yankee customs make more sense," she said, hoisting it onto Bonnet's back. "You ought to try it, Violet.''

Violet looked shocked; then a slow grin came over her face. A look of mischief sparkled in her amber eyes. "I must be plumb crazy . . . but I believe I will. To tell the honest truth, I've always wanted to. It's never seemed fair to me that men should have the freedom to do as they please, while we must suffer simply for the sake of propriety.''

A wild thought occurred to Ashley. Mom said that Violet had bucked tradition by refusing to ride sidesaddle. Could I have been responsible for liberating Violet? Wow, wouldn't that be weird!

Suddenly it seemed perfectly natural for Ashley to raise her fist over her head and cry, "Right on!" It was one of Lou's old sixties sayings, but it fit the occasion.

Violet copied her gesture. "Ride on!" she echoed mistakenly, flipping her brother's saddle onto Lafayette's back.

Ashley decided not to correct her. Some things were better off left alone.

They had ridden for more than a mile, through shady

groves and past cotton fields that seemed to stretch on forever, when Violet brought her cantering horse to a sudden halt. From where they stood, at the top of a hill looking out over the countryside, Ashley watched a doll-sized carriage pulled by a pair of sleek bays making its way up the meandering road to Oakehurst in a cloud of red dust.

Violet moaned softly. When Ashley glanced over, she saw that Violet had turned ghostly pale.

"That's Wade Calvert's carriage!" she cried. "And he's headed straight for Oakehurst! Oh, Ashley, what am I going to do?"

A hard lump of desperation formed in Ashley's stomach. This could only mean one thing. That Wade Calvert was determined to ask for Violet's hand in marriage, even though she despised him.

"I think you should try talking to your father again," Ashley said. "Let him know how you feel. If he really loves you, he won't make you marry Mr. Calvert."

"But you don't understand." Violet turned an anguished gaze on Ashley. Her hair, tousled from the ride, blew haphazardly about her face, giving Ashley the eerie feeling for an instant that she was looking at a reflection of herself. "Papa feels that Mr. Calvert would be by far the best match for me. I'd live in a grand house with lots of slaves. I'd have everything except"—she sniffled—"*Elliot.*" She began to weep.

Ashley felt so helpless. She had to think of something quick. But what?

"I . . . I could try talking to your father myself," she offered. "Maybe I could explain it in a different way, so he'd see how impossible it is."

"I don't think it would do any good," Violet said. "After all, you're Elliot's sister."

"No, I'm n— I mean, well, yeah, but it couldn't hurt to try." Whew! That had been close. She'd almost spilled the beans.

A tiny spark of hope glimmered in Violet's eyes. "Oh,

Ash, if you could . . . well, you—you'd be saving my *life!*"

Mine, too, Ashley added silently, feeling a lot less hopeful than she'd sounded.

"Miss Beaumont, I presume? I'm afraid I haven't had the pleasure. I'm Wade Calvert—p'raps Violet has spoken of me to you?"

Ashley stared into a pair of eyes so black and bottomless she had an instant's sensation of dizziness, like looking down the mouth of a well. She found herself instinctively taking a step backward.

Just our luck, running into him like this! she thought. She and Violet were on their way back from the stable when they'd practically bumped into Mr. Calvert stepping down from his carriage.

Now those bottomless black eyes were fixed on Violet, and his mouth stretched in a thin smile of triumph. "Miss Violet. You're looking prettier than ever." He didn't say what the purpose of his visit was, but from the possessive way he was looking at Violet, there was no doubt in Ashley's mind what his intentions were.

Ashley couldn't have said exactly why Wade Calvert made her skin crawl. He wasn't ugly or misshapen. There was just something so . . . well, creepy about him. Those cold eyes, and that oily voice. Up close, his face was grainy and coarse. She tried not to imagine what it would feel like to have those thick hands touching her. Ugh! No wonder Violet wanted to avoid him.

Ashley was proud of the way Violet contained herself. Except for the color that rose up her creamy neck to form mottled spots of red in her cheeks, she gave no indication of how she felt toward Mr. Calvert. Keeping a cool distance, she merely nodded in his direction.

"Good morning, Mr. Calvert," she greeted him stiffly. "If you've come to pay a call on Papa, I'm afraid he's not here. You see, he stayed the night at Fairfield." Violet's amber eyes glittered with triumph.

Not much of a victory, Ashley thought in despair. If Mr. Calvert wants to marry Violet, he's not going to let a small thing like that stop him.

But Mr. Calvert only smiled, completely unruffled. "But you don't understand. Your father is with me."

A noise behind Ashley caused her to whirl about in time to see Papa Oakes stepping down from the carriage.

"Wade was kind enough to bring me home." Papa Oakes beamed at Violet as he straightened his hat and smoothed his ruffled cravat. "And we've had a most interesting discussion, which I'll speak to you about later in private, my dear. Aren't you forgetting your manners? Why haven't you invited our good friend Mr. Calvert inside?"

Violet stared at him, shocked. There was clearly no doubt in her mind now that her father had given his consent for the marriage. All the color drained from her face, leaving her a deathly ashen color.

She opened her mouth to speak. "I—" But no words would come out. With a choked cry, she spun about and fled into the house.

Ashley stared after Violet, a wave of despair crashing over her. *Now what?*

Chapter Nine

DUMB. DUMB. DUMB.

You are so dumb, Ashley berated herself. How could you think for one minute that Papa Oakes would listen to anything you had to say?

She closed the door to her room and sank down wearily on the bed. It had been a complete disaster, her confrontation with the stern Papa Oakes downstairs a few minutes ago.

Maybe if she'd planned it out better . . .

But there wasn't time. Desperation had forced her to speak out.

Waiting only until Mr. Calvert was gone, she'd burst without knocking into the library, where Papa Oakes sat calmly at his enormous carved desk puffing on his pipe. "Please, Mr. Oakes, please don't force Violet to marry Mr. Calvert!" she'd pleaded.

Glancing up from the papers spread in front of him, he had fixed her with an angry glare.

"I'll thank you to mind your own affairs, Miss Beaumont," he'd said. "Whoever Violet marries, it's no concern of yours."

"But it *is*," she'd insisted. Frustration burned and twisted inside her. If only she could tell the truth! But he would never believe her. She would have about as much chance of convincing Papa Oakes she was his great-great-great-granddaughter as she would convincing him that slavery was wrong. "I mean . . . well, I—I've come to think a lot of Violet, and I care about her happiness. Oh, Mr. Oakes, don't you see? She doesn't *love* Mr. Calvert.''

"Love has very little to do with it," he said. "Only fools marry for love. I intend to see that Violet is well looked after by a man of good background and solid standing. If you've come here to speak on behalf of your brother, I'm afraid you're wasting your time.''

"I'm not here because of Elliot. I'm here to warn you that you'll be doing a terrible thing if you force Violet to marry Mr. Calvert.'' The words came pouring from her in a hot rush. "Not just to Violet, but—but to whole generations of Beaumonts who will never get born. A hundred years from now, you could have a redheaded granddaughter just like Violet, and she—'' Ashley stopped herself.

Oh, God, had she really said that? But there, it was out. And it was so good to speak the truth for a change, even if it wasn't the whole truth. Ashley had felt as if she'd been zipped inside a suitcase all this time, and suddenly she was outside, breathing the fresh air, stretching her arms and legs. Oh, how she wished she could make them all understand!

But Papa Oakes hadn't understood. He'd dismissed her with a wave of his hand, as if she were a deranged servant.

And now she was back where she'd started. Which was exactly nowhere.

Ashley wriggled out of the riding boots Violet had lent her, and flopped back onto the soft goosedown pillows. The late morning sunshine sifting through the trees outside formed a lacy pattern on the blue carpet. It was so hot. Even with the window open. The air was like honey, sweet-smelling and gooey. She felt sticky all over, and it made her tired just to breathe. To think she'd always taken air conditioners for granted!

From the room next door came the muffled sounds of Violet sobbing her heart out. Poor Violet! Ashley had tried to console her, but there was nothing she could say to make Violet feel better.

A wave of exhaustion swept over her. I'll rest for just a

few minutes, she told herself. I can't think right now, but maybe after a while I'll come up with another plan.

For some reason, she found herself thinking about Dorothy in *The Wizard of Oz,* and how she'd searched all over Oz for the way back to Kansas, when all along it was right there in the ruby slippers she had on her feet.

A lump formed in her throat. If only it could be that easy for me!

Ashley felt asleep imagining she was wearing those same ruby slippers. All she had to do was click the heels together three times, and she would be transported back home to Westdale . . .

"Ashley!"

Ashley heard a banging noise. Someone was calling her name. It sounded far away and distorted, like sounds heard underwater. She struggled to reach the surface, but it was like swimming in a sea of gray cotton.

Gradually her head began to clear. The banging grew louder.

"Violet?" she muttered thickly, realizing she'd slept longer than she intended.

"Ashley! What on earth is going on in there?"

It wasn't Violet calling her. It was her mother.

With a sharp jolt, Ashley came fully awake. Gone was the soft feather quilt she'd been lying on at Oakehurst. She was on the floor of her own room in Westdale.

Ashley felt as if the air had been knocked from her lungs.

"Holy moly!" she gasped.

Is this real?

Or am I dreaming?

She jumped to her feet, but the floor rocked beneath her, and she had to clutch the edge of her desk to keep from falling. Her head spun, and her legs felt rubbery, as if she'd just taken a ride on a roller coaster.

Maybe this is real, and the whole time trip to Oakehurst was a dream.

Then she looked down, and gave a startled little squeak.

She was still wearing Violet's riding habit! She fingered the dark brown velvet in wonder. Bubbles of hysteria fizzled and popped in her throat.

I was there, she thought. I really did go back in time!

And it feels like I've been gone a hundred years.

A deep boom rattled the window. The room was lit by a strobe flash of lightning. It was storming—just as it had been when she'd left.

Ashley snatched the digital clock from the bookshelf above her desk. She'd left at four o'clock on Friday. The liquid crystal display showed that it was now two minutes past—still on Friday! Her mind whirled with confusion.

That's impossible! I was gone two whole days. Not just two minutes. My clock must have stopped. Something went haywire with its circuits.

But the numbers shifted to read 4:03 as she watched the display.

And nothing had changed. Everything was exactly where she'd left it. Her clothes and backpack piled on the floor of her closet. The dress Mom had gotten her tossed across the bed. No one had been in here. There were no signs that the police had combed her room for clues.

And the storm . . .

Something winked at her, and Ashley looked down to find Boo-Boo's one remaining glass eye gazing at her with a knowing expression. She snatched him up, burying her face against his rough mangy fur.

"Oh, Boo-Boo, is this for real?" she whispered. "Am I really home?"

"Ashley!" The doorknob rattled. "For heaven's sake, if you're in there . . ."

Her mother!

"Sorry, Mom!" Ashley called out. "I—I didn't hear you. I was busy." She couldn't believe how normal she sounded. As if she weren't trembling from head to toe. As if this were just another ordinary day. As if she hadn't just come back from a two-day trip to another century.

"Just checking," Mom said. "The electricity went out

for a couple of seconds a few minutes ago. I wanted to make sure everything was okay up here."

"Oh, fine. Everything's just fine."

"Well, okay . . . just don't get too caught up in whatever you're doing. I could use some help with dinner."

"Sure, Mom. I'll be down in a few minutes." She was aware that words were coming from her mouth, but it was as if someone else were talking.

She waited to hear the soft tread of her mother's footsteps descending the stairs, then let out her breath in a long trembling rush.

So it's true, she thought. No one missed me. I've only been gone for a couple of minutes. But how is that possible?

Ashley turned on her computer and punched the keys to reactivate her fractal program. She stared at the glowing green equations on the screen.

It took her about ten minutes to figure out what had gone wrong. One of her equations was off by a decibel of 0.0243. That meant that two minutes in the present equaled *two whole days* in the past!

The closest Ashley could come to imagining it was to picture the past and the present as two intersecting lines. The mistake in her equation had caused the tiniest crack to separate those lines.

"And I fell between the crack," she whispered to herself in amazement.

Ashley understood now what had happened when she'd zapped her teddy bear into the past. What had seemed like only a couple of minutes to her had really been more like two days for Boo-Boo. And all that time she'd worried about being stuck in the nineteenth century, almost no time had elapsed in the present!

The last piece to the puzzle fell into place. When she'd gone back to Oakehurst, she'd discovered the door to time, but now she had the key. And that meant . . .

. . . *I could go back and forth if I wanted, and no one would miss me!*

96

According to her calculations, the crack in time would apply to the past as well. So she could go back to Oakehurst after two days in the present, and no one there would miss her, either.

Oakehurst. Ashley's stomach dropped, as if she had just shot up twenty floors in a very fast elevator. She was so deliriously happy to be home that the thought of going back to the past filled her with terror.

But what about Violet?

If it don't go back . . . if I don't find some way of helping her . . . she'll have to marry Mr. Calvert.

And then I won't be . . .

No. I won't think about that right now. For the moment, I'm safe—and I'm home.

Ashley struggled with the miniature buttons and hooks of her velvet jacket and riding skirt. All she wanted to do right now was take a long hot shower and climb into her oldest pair of jeans and her baggiest sweatshirt. Then go downstairs and guzzle a king-sized Pepsi.

Tonight she was just going to enjoy being back in the twentieth century. She was going to treat herself to all the marvelous things she'd never appreciated before. TV. Telephone. Hot running water. The list was endless. But it seemed to Ashley as if they'd all just been invented.

Her stomach continued to flip-flop excitedly.

"Tomorrow," she whispered to Merlin, stealing one of Scarlett O'Hara's best lines. "I'll think about Oakehurst tomorrow."

Chapter Ten

ASHLEY STARED AT HERSELF IN THE MIRROR with a sinking heart.

No, pink was definitely not her color. And this dress, with all its ruffles, made her look like an ostrich. She stared in dismay at her spindly legs protruding below the flounced hem. How am I going to face Len at the picnic looking like this? she wondered.

She didn't even *want* to go to the picnic. In fact, she'd forgotten all about it until her mother had poked her head in this morning while she was still in bed, chirping, "Rise and shine, sleepyhead! The sun's out, so the picnic's on. And I can't wait to see you in your new dress. You'll be the prettiest girl there."

Ashley had been dreaming she was back at Oakehurst, and was shocked to see her own mother instead of Violet standing there, dressed in spotless white slacks and a pretty turquoise blouse tied at the waist with a colorful silk scarf.

"Coming, Mom," she'd mumbled.

Now, even after a hot shower and breakfast, she still didn't feel as if her head was screwed on right. Her thoughts kept returning to Oakehurst . . . and Violet.

Poor Violet! What will happen to her if I don't go back and find a way to help her? She'll be forced to marry Mr. Calvert, and be miserable for the rest of her life.

And what about us—Mom, Andy, and me? If Violet marries the wrong man, then all those generations of Beaumonts won't get born. Including us. And if we cease to exist, then—

What? The prospect was both terrifying and mind-boggling.

Will we simply fade into nothingness?

Ashley began to shiver despite the sun that streamed in through the rain-spotted window, filling the room with its buttery glow. No, she thought. I'm imagining things. I've seen too many movies. That couldn't happen to us.

The sound of splashing water drew her to the window, where she had a bird's-eye view of her father washing the family station wagon in the driveway. The sun gleamed on the dark blue metal and the bald spot on top of his head. He was whistling as he pushed his soapy rag in circular strokes across the windshield.

An ache formed in Ashley's throat. She hadn't appreciated Dad enough. He didn't often say a lot, but he was always there, solid and dependable. She remembered the time she'd come home crying because she'd gotten a D on her report card. Dad had told her, in his quiet, uncritical way, that you could look at a D two ways: as an excuse to give up . . . or a challenge to do better. And after that, she'd tried harder and was able to bring her mark up two whole grades by the following semester.

Ashley tried to imagine how Dad would feel if he came home from work one day to an empty house, to find that his wife and daughter didn't exist anymore.

Ashley covered her face with her hands. What a dumb thing to imagine! I'm not going anywhere, and neither is Mom! she told herself vehemently.

Back at Oakehurst she'd let her imagination run wild, because everything had seemed so strange and unreal. Thoughts about disappearing into thin air were no weirder than what was going on right under her nose. But here, in Westdale, she was back on solid ground again. Everything was so *normal.* Her father washing the car, and her mom was downstairs packing the sweet-potato pies she'd made for the picnic. The thought of something a hundred years in the past affecting her now seemed as far-out at this moment as a flying saucer landing on the front lawn.

But in spite of all her rationalizations, Ashley couldn't make the coldness inside her go away. She felt as if there were a lump of ice cream in her stomach that refused to melt. Horrible thoughts kept seeping in: *What if I'm not making all this up? What if, by going back in time, I knocked a screw loose or something? History could change, couldn't it? The whole Beaumont branch of the family tree could be erased . . .*

But I couldn't go back to Oakehurst to try to fix things right now, even if I wanted to, she reminded herself. *Since the mistake in my fractal program holds true for the past as well as the present, then I still have almost two whole days before the crack in time closes enough to allow me to return to Violet's. She probably doesn't even know I'm gone!*

With a sigh, Ashley returned to the full-length mirror on her closet door. Didn't she have enough problems in the present without worrying herself into knots over Violet? Like how she was going to wear this dress to the picnic without making a complete fool of herself in front of everyone, especially Len!

Oh, Violet, I wish you could be here, Ashley thought. *You would know what to do. I have to wear this dress if I don't want to hurt Mom's feelings, but I just know you'd somehow find a way to make it okay.*

Suddenly, it was as if Violet was standing right beside her, whispering confidences in her ear. Ashley could almost hear her lilting Southern drawl: *Land sakes, Ash, straighten those shoulders and hold your head up. You don't want those boys thinking you're the retiring type, do you?*

Ashley smiled. Of course! If Violet had to wear something she looked awful in, she'd do it with as much style as possible. And probably carry it off, too.

If I go slinking off to that picnic looking as embarrassed as I feel, then I might as well be wearing a neon sign flashing "Wimp!" Violet would have the right idea. Since I have to wear this dress, I might as well do it with style.

An idea popped into her head.

Ashley wrenched open the door to her closet and pulled down a cardboard box from the top shelf. It's got to be here somewhere, she thought, rummaging among a jumble of old school playbills and photos, Girl Scout badges, the tinfoil crown she'd worn as a fairy in her sixth-grade play. There. She pounced upon a pink ostrich boa. She'd bought it at a thrift shop and had worn it to Lou's Halloween party the previous year, dressed as Auntie Mame. It was on the ratty side, but when she'd draped it over her shoulders, the pink dress from Brigitte's was transformed from hideous to Cyndi Lauper funky.

Giggling with delight, Ashley dug into her jewelry box and added a pair of dangly rhinestone earrings and a long strand of Day-Glo pop beads. Next, she found a can of mousse and used a handful of the foamy lather to spike her hair. She stood back to survey the results in the mirror.

Wild! Violet wouldn't recognize me, she thought, but I have a feeling she'd approve.

"Love your outfit." Bif O'Neill smiled down at Ashley with surprised approval.

Ashley had to tip her head back to meet Bif's gaze. He was at least two heads taller than the next tallest person at the picnic. People at O. Henry joked that Bif didn't just play on the basketball team, he *was* the team. Everybody knew who Bif was, but Ashley was surprised that he was talking to her. He sat near her in English, but they'd never exchanged two words before this. Maybe it was because they were at the company picnic, her *father*'s company, and Bif felt he had to be nice. His mother was one of Conn-Tech's quality-control supervisors.

Ashley was so ruffled by Bif's unexpected attention, and so busy staring up, up, up at him, that she didn't notice until it was almost too late that she'd let her paper plate tip too far forward.

Bif's lanky arm shot out, catching the edge of the plate just as her barbecued chicken drumstick was about to roll onto the toes of his boat-sized Pumas. Ashley was horrified, but Bif's gray green eyes merely danced with amusement.

"Thanks," she muttered. A slow fire of humiliation crept through her. Just once, couldn't she talk to a boy without tripping or dropping something?

Bif didn't seem bothered, though. "Good thing I have snap reflexes," he said, laughing. "You have to in basketball, or you spend all your time on the bench. Ever been to one of our games?"

"Uh . . . no." Brilliant. He's going to think my entire vocabulary consists of about five words.

Ashley dropped her gaze to the lump of blackened chicken on her plate, feeling her appetite shrivel. Oh, what's the use? I'd never be able to hold his interest, anyway . . .

Then suddenly, as if Violet had jabbed her between the shoulder blades, Ashley straightened, remembering Violet's advice, *Show interest in a boy, and he'll be interested in you.* How could she have forgotten? It had worked at the Fairfield barbecue, why couldn't it work now?

Ashley lifted her chin and took a good look at Bif for the first time. She'd been so busy worrying about what he thought of her, she hadn't noticed what nice eyes he had, or how blond his hair was.

She smiled, feeling less nervous than before. "I don't know much about basketball, but I'll bet it's fascinating."

Bif beamed as if she'd just handed him a trophy. "Let me explain how it works . . ." he began, launching into a detailed analysis of the game.

Ashley stared at the Adam's apple bobbing up and down in his skinny neck, only half-listening to his words. See, that wasn't so hard, she told herself. And you did it all by yourself, without having to pretend you were Scarlett O'Hara. Maybe there's hope for you, after all . . .

Out of the corner of her eye, Ashley searched the crowd

gathered on the town green, where her father held the picnic every year. Had Len arrived yet? She hadn't seen him. But there were so many people, it was hard to tell.

She scanned the area she and Bif were standing in, near the food tables, which were clustered under an open-sided orange-and-white-striped parachute tent. No Len. He wasn't at the picnic tables, either. Or standing in line in front of the barbecue grills over by the fence.

Why do I even care? Ashley wondered. She told herself that if she knew where he was, then she could avoid him . . . and avoid making a fool of herself in front of him again. Okay, so she'd managed all right with Bif. But she didn't have a crush on Bif, so it wasn't all that hard.

On the other hand, she told herself, you'd be pretty hard to miss in this outfit. Admit it—you *want* Len to notice you. You're *hoping* he'll speak to you . . .

Stupid. Why couldn't she just accept the fact that Len would never be interested in her? Why should he, when he could have Alicia?

She forced her mind back to what Bif was saying. " . . . and then with the game in the final minute, Rick Spafford—he plays center, you know—set me up for the most incredible slam-dunk you've ever seen. It was"—the glazed expression in his eyes shifted, and he focused on Ashley once again—"well, you had to be there, I guess."

"I wish I had been." Ashley smiled harder, feeling a twinge of guilt that she hadn't been paying more attention. "It really sounds exciting."

Bif shifted from one foot to the other, looking pleased and sheepish. "Well, maybe you'd like to come watch me play sometime." He was staring at her with new interest. "You know, it's funny. We're in the same class, but we never really talked. I guess I'm sort of the shy type. And I thought you were too . . . until I saw you in that awesome outfit."

Ashley's confidence shot up several more notches. Waves of warmth rippled through her, radiating from a glowing point in the pit of her stomach. Bif didn't think she was hopeless. He liked the way she looked, too. Maybe there's really nothing wrong with me. Maybe all I needed was a little push in the right direction.

Violet gave me that push.

Will I be able to help Violet?

Oh, no, I can't think about that right now or I'll go crazy, Ashley told herself. I've got to concentrate on—

Len! As she spotted him, Ashley felt as if she'd been zapped by a jolt of electricity. There he was, sauntering past a row of picnic tables, looking as cool as could be in his stone-washed jeans and a tank top that showed off his muscles. Her heart jumped into overdrive. Oh, Len, if only you knew . . .

As if her thoughts were sending out little radar blips, Len's head swiveled slowly in her direction, his face expressionless, his eyes hidden behind a pair of Ray-ban sunglasses.

Ashley felt herself shriveling, curling up at the edges like a leaf. Len is probably laughing at me. He's probably wondering what new stunt this is, whether I'll wear the punch bowl on my head next.

Oh, God, he's heading in this direction! He'll probably smirk and say. "Yo, Ashley, way to go." Just like before, when I did that kamikaze dive into those desks.

She had to escape. Fast.

Ashley quickly set her plate down on the nearest table. "Listen, Bif, it's been great talking to you, but I . . . I promised my mother I'd help her with the pies."

Before Bif could protest, Ashley made a beeline for the crowded safety of the food tent. She spotted her mom at the far end of the dessert table, serving up wedges of sweet-potato pie and spritzing each one with a perfect white dollop of whipped cream.

"I could do that, Mom," Ashley said. "Why don't you take a break?"

Eugenie looked up at her daughter. "Oh, I don't mind, sugar. Besides, you should be out there having fun with your friends." She paused, the can of whipped cream frozen in midair, a smile spreading across her face as she gazed at something over Ashley's shoulder. In an exaggerated whisper, she added, "I see one now . . . he's right behind you. And I don't think it's my sweet-potato pie he's interested in."

Ashley whirled about in alarm. Had Bif followed her? *Wham!*

She was struck by a thousand volts of electricity, coming straight at her from a pair of dark green brown eyes. Len! His sunglasses were pushed up on top of his head, and—there was no mistaking it—he was staring right at her.

Ashley felt as if she were paralyzed. Her body tingled all over, as if she had become a conduit for the electricity, but she was unable to move.

He was walking toward her. Please, she prayed, please don't let me make a fool of myself. Just this once . . .

If only her stomach would stop doing gymnastics. If only she could wipe this stupid frozen smile off her face. If only—

"Yo, Ashley, how's it going? Great outfit—it's really cool."

His words seemed to drift at her like bubbles from a soap wand, tiny cool kisses breaking against her cheeks and forehead. I'm not dreaming this, am I?

Up close, Ashley noticed Len had a small moon-shaped scar on his temple, just above his right eyebrow. And there was the tiniest gap between his front teeth. His eyes, dark green shot through with splinters of gold brown, held her gaze without flickering off to the side. Ashley felt as if she were pinned under a microscope.

"I wanted to try something different," she found herself saying. Laughter bubbled up from the pool of nervousness in her stomach.

Len nodded, smiling as if she'd said something really amusing. "Yeah? Well, I'm not surprised. I had you figured as the wild-and-crazy type."

Ashley stared at him, bewildered. "Me? Are you sure you don't have me mixed up with someone else?"

105

His smile widened. "Who else comes into class like Reggie Jackson sliding into home plate? No kidding, that first time I saw you, I thought—"

"Here"—Ashley grabbed a plate of pie and thrust it at Len—"have some dessert." Anything to get off this embarrassing subject. Oh, God, why did he have to remind her? "My mother made it," she said.

Len forked in a mouthful of golden custardy pie. "Delicious. Your mom's a great cook."

"It's an old Southern recipe. It's been in our family for generations." She thought about Violet, and the confidence she'd felt with Bif began seeping back in.

Without thinking about what she was doing, Ashley grabbed an empty paper plate from the stack beside her and began fanning herself, as if she'd been transported, in the blink of an eye, back to the barbecue at Fairfield.

"You hot or something?" Len asked.

Ashley froze, staring down at the paper plate in her hand. In her mind, she'd been fluttering a delicate ivory-handled lace fan. She dropped the plate as if it had suddenly grown too hot to handle.

"Uh . . . no. I mean, yeah, well, it is a little warm." Warm? She felt like those chickens being barbecued on the grill.

Len winked. "Must be that hot Southern blood of yours."

Is he—it seemed like—no, it couldn't be—*is he flirting with me?*

Ashley stiffened. Maybe he was just doing it for kicks. Or charity. Be Nice to a Nerd Day. She thought about the colored bracelets sliding up Alicia's arm as she snaked it through Len's. Why would Len have anything to do with me when he's got Alicia?

"It—it looks like we're going to have a late fall this year," she said, struggling to make this sound as if it were just a normal conversation.

They had moved out from under the tent and stood gazing up at a huge old maple tree. The grass below it was scattered with only a few gold and scarlet leaves. She could see the Indian summer stretching ahead, long walks in the country with Len, holding hands, dry leaves crunching underfoot. Sitting on the dock at the lake, talking quietly, jeans rolled up, the icy water lapping their toes. Riding their bikes to school, their breath forming little puffs of white vapor in the crisp air.

Stop it, she commanded herself, *stop torturing yourself.*

"That's what I like about living here," Len replied thoughtfully. "Nothing ever gets rushed. Not like New York City. You know what it's like being crammed into a subway car at rush hour with a hundred other people all hustling to get somewhere? The only time it slows down is when something breaks down or gets stuck."

Ashley smiled, thinking back to the leisurely pace at Oakehurst. What would Len make of that? She imagined what his reaction would be if she told him about her journey back in time.

By the way, Len, I just got back from a trip to the Civil War period . . .

Yo, Ashley, I always knew you were the wild-and-crazy type.

She stifled a giggle at her imagined conversation and pulled her attention back to the real Len. "I can't imagine growing up in New York. I've lived in Westdale all my life."

As she gazed at Len, it was as if she'd always seen him in black-and-white and now she was seeing him in vivid Technicolor. His dark lashes were brushed with gold at the ends, she noticed. Dark red crescents of sunburn marked the high ridges of his cheekbones. His skin was a smooth olive color, except where the faint peppering of a beard shadowed his angular jaw.

"I can't imagine you anywhere else, either," Len said softly. He bent down, plucking a flame-colored leaf from the grass. Smiling, he held it against her hair, his knuckles brushing her cheek. "You see? Perfect match."

Ashley's heart seemed to fly right out of her. Len's touch

107

had left a blaze of warmth across her cheek. She wanted to press her hand against it, keeping it there always. She would never wash her cheek again.

She couldn't think of a thing to say. Quick. Anything. "Want some more pie?" Her voice came out a rusty croak.

Len glanced down at the half-eaten piece on his plate. "No thanks. I have a ways to go yet on this one. Hey, how come you're not eating any?"

"Me? Oh, I'm pretty full. Besides, once I get started on Mom's pie, there's no stopping me. If I didn't watch out, I'd turn into the Goodyear blimp."

Len laughed. "I don't see much danger of that happening."

Ashley could have kicked herself. He probably thinks you're fishing for compliments, dope.

"You like baseball?" Len asked, forking in another bite of pie.

She remembered how Bif had perked up when she'd shown an interest in basketball. She nodded. "Sure."

"Great! I'm getting a game together for later this afternoon, after everyone's had a chance to digest their food. You want to be on my team?"

Ashley's heart sank. So that's why he'd followed her and spent all this time talking to her. He was recruiting players for his team. That was all.

"I'm not very good," Ashley said in a small voice. In her mind, she saw herself at last year's picnic, striking out for the third time with all the bases loaded. She couldn't chance a replay of that fiasco this year. Not in front of Len.

"Oh, hey, it doesn't matter," Len tried to reassure her. "It's just for fun. What do you say?"

Tears of disappointment pricked her eyes. She ducked her head so he wouldn't see. She'd been hoping . . . Oh, never mind. It was crazy for her to have thought Len might really be interested.

"I really don't think so, Len," she muttered, clenching her fists to keep from crying as she stared down at her

108

peach-frosted toenails peeking out from under her sandal straps. Stupid feet. They'd just trip her up again. She'd ruin the whole game. Why couldn't he see that? "I—I have to leave early," she added lamely. A dumb excuse. Her father was the host of the picnic, so their family was always the last to leave.

Len's face closed up, became expressionless. He pulled his Ray-bans down over his eyes again, so all Ashley could see when she looked at him were two dark mirrors reflecting twin images of her own miserable face.

"Suit yourself." He turned with a nonchalant little shrug, as if to say, *Hey, no big deal, I was only asking to be polite, anyway.* He started to walk away, then paused to call back over his shoulder, "Yo, Ashley, if you change your mind, just let me know."

She smiled weakly and lifted her hand in an apologetic little wave.

But Len didn't see. His back was to her as he strode off in the direction of the picnic tables.

I blew it, Ashley thought, misery forming a hard lump in the little hollow just below her rib cage. And I'm not even exactly sure how.

Oh, Violet, she cried silently. *How can I untangle your love life, when I can't even seem to stop screwing up mine?*

Chapter Eleven

"I'LL NEVER HAVE A BOYFRIEND," LOU GREEN-span sighed dramatically as she peeled the wrapper from a sandwich the size of a breadbox.

Ashley nodded absently as she gazed across the campus lawn, bustling with the lunchtime crowd. She was only half-tuned in to what Lou was saying. It had been like that all morning in her classes, too. Her teachers might have been talking in some ancient Assyrian dialect as far as she was concerned.

My body might be in the twentieth century, Ashley concluded, but my head is still back in 1861.

Lou was peering at her. "Did you hear what I just said?"

Ashley struggled to brush away the cobwebs her brain seemed to be wrapped in. "Huh? Oh, yeah, I'm listening."

Lou didn't let up. "Are you sure? You know, you've been acting really spacey lately. Like you're on another planet or something. Is everything okay with you?"

"Uh-huh . . . fine," Ashley lied.

She longed to tell Lou about her discovery, but this was hardly the kind of thing you dropped in casual conversation. Lou would think she had totally flipped out! And now certainly wasn't the right time to break the news. Not with the whole school milling around them, and Tina sitting beside Lou. I'll tell Lou later, Ashley decided, after I've had a chance to sort out the whole confusing mess myself so I can explain it to her without sounding like a lunatic.

110

Ashley's thoughts were interrupted by Lou, who commanded Tina Scott in a deep voice, "Beam her down, Scottie."

Ashley cracked a smile despite herself. Lou didn't look the least bit like Captain Kirk. In her baggy overalls and tie-dyed T-shirt, with a bandana wrapped about her frizzy blond hair, she looked more like a throwback to the sixties.

Tina went along with the gag. In a fake Scottish brogue she quipped, "I'll do my best, Capt'n Kirrrrk. But I'm havin' trouble with the transporter. That Klingon ship off the starrrboard is blockin' the channels." She broke off with a laugh. "You see? I do watch something besides *Love Boat.*"

Tina's laugh startled Ashley, as it always did. It was deep and husky, not at all what you'd expect from someone only four feet eleven who looked like Tinkerbell. But then Tina was full of surprises and contradictions. Despite her size, she had more spunk and energy than anyone Ashley knew.

Ashley recalled the mountain of aluminum cans Tina had collected last year during O. Henry's recycling drive. It was taller than she was and twice what anyone else had brought in. And what about the time Tina had stood up to that subsitute PE teacher who had been making fun of Ashley's attempts at the breast stroke in front of the whole class? Ashley would never forget how Tina had popped up out of the water as if jet-propelled, her pixie face bright with indignation.

"Some people who call themselves teachers shouldn't be allowed within ten miles of a school!" she'd cried.

Ashley had been grateful to Tina for leaping to her defense that way, and they'd been friends ever since.

She looked over at Tina now, smiling to herself. Tina was wearing culottes and a Smurf T-shirt, her wispy blond hair pulled back with a bright yellow butterfly clip. She often complained that she couldn't find clothes that fit her in the junior department, so she was stuck with children's sizes.

111

Who would ever guess that little Tina was really "Dear Dolly," savvy adviser to the lovelorn, whose column in the *O. Henry Herald* was eagerly awaited from week to week by everyone from the lowliest freshmen to the most jaded seniors? No one. Only the *Herald*'s staff and Tina's closest friends knew her secret identity.

That was another funny thing about Tina, Ashley reflected. She had patched up more relationships and brought more couples together than Cupid himself, yet she was dead set against falling in love herself. It didn't make sense. But Tina seldom talked about it, and Ashley didn't want to pry.

Right now I could use some of Dolly's advice to help me sort out the mess I'm in, she thought. Tina would probably know what to do about Violet and Mr. Calvert . . . if I could ever get her to believe my crazy story.

She switched back to what Lou had been saying instead. "Speaking of boyfriends, I'm not exactly an expert in that department myself." She looked over at Tina with a smile. "Unlike *some* people I know."

Tina threw up her hands. "Okay, okay. I'm the expert, but in my case it's all talk and no action." She grew thoughtful all of a sudden, staring down at the grass. "Anyway, I don't have time for a boyfriend. I'm too busy trying to straighten out everybody else's romances." Her words sounded hollow to Ashley, but she didn't comment.

"Well, my date last night was a total bummer," Lou said, looking glum. "The minute I open my mouth, people of the male persuasion automatically run in the other direction."

"Come on, Lou," Ashley said. "It's not that bad, and it's not because they don't like you. It's . . ." She tried to find the right way of putting it without hurting Lou's feelings.

"What?" Lou interrupted, going off the deep end in typical Lou fashion. "Do I have two heads or something? Or is it my breath? Maybe I should switch to another toothpaste."

112

Ashley tried to keep a straight face, and she could see that Tina was having trouble, too. Ashley knew that even though Lou was making jokes about her plight, she was really upset. Ashley hardly ever saw her this way. Lou was usually pretty confident. She must really be shook up about that date, Ashley thought.

She patted Lou's plump knee. "There's nothing wrong with you, Lou. It's just that, well, when you go on about the sixties, I'm sure a lot of guys just don't know what you're talking about."

Lou's expression turned sheepish. "Yeah, I guess I do get sort of carried away sometimes. Last night . . . well, it wasn't all Doug's fault. We sort of got into this argument."

"Argument?" Tina arched an eyebrow.

"About the Doors." Lou took a bite from her submarine sandwich.

"What could you possibly find to disagree on about doors?" Ashley wanted to know.

Lou shot her a disgusted look. "Not doors. *The Doors*. They were only one of the greatest bands that ever rocked. But Doug said whoever they were, they couldn't hold a candle to Bruce Springsteen."

Tina stretched out her legs, leaning back against a sturdy maple tree, its branches laden with crimson leaves. She stared at Lou, her enormous blue eyes seeming to take up half her face. "Well, if it's just a difference in musical tastes—"

"It's more than that!" Lou shot back. "I feel like I was born in the wrong generation. All the things I like no one else our age can relate to—things like peace, love, tie-dyed T-shirts, Moby Grape . . ."

"Moby Grape?" Tina's eyes grew even wider.

Ashley nudged her, murmuring, "Don't ask."

Lou sighed deeply, replacing her half-eaten sandwich in her lunch bag. Wow, she must really be depressed, Ashley thought. That's the first time I've ever seen Lou leave part of her lunch. It usually took a tragedy of major proportions

113

to make Lou lose her appetite, like the time she heard a rumor that the Grateful Dead was disbanding.

"I wish," Lou said, "I could find someone, a boy, like *me*. Someone who understands. Who doesn't think Santana is some kind of suntan lotion. Who wears tie-dyed T-shirts . . . no, has a tie-dyed *soul*."

"You could always advertise," offered Tina matter-of-factly.

Ashley laughed, thinking it must be a joke. Then she realized Tina was serious.

"Advertise?" Lou was incredulous. "You mean like those ads you see in the Personals?" She affected a dreamy pose, clasping her hands below her chin. " 'Looking for nonsmoking nature lover to share sunsets with, hikes in the woods, and to rub calamine lotion on my poison ivy and mosquito bites . . .' "

That forced a giggle out of Tina. "Okay, okay, make a joke out of it, but I'm serious. Lots of people find their perfect match that way. My mom has a friend who met her husband through the Personals. They're both dentists, and they're crazy about each other."

"Sounds like a perfect match, all right," Ashley remarked. "They can check each other out for cavities."

Lou looked thoughtful as she brushed halfheartedly at the crumbs sprinkled across the bib of her overalls.

"You know," she said, "maybe you have something there, Tina. After all, what have I got to lose? No one would even know it was me. I could place an ad in the *Sentinel* and give a post office box for my return address . . ." An expression of hope lit her round face. "Hey, it might even work!"

Tina shrugged modestly. "Don't mention it. It's all in the line of duty." She pulled a notebook from her orange nylon backpack, flipped it open to a clean page, and grabbed a pencil. "Now let's come up with an ad. Anybody got any ideas?"

"How about 'Desperately Seeking Sixties Lover'?" Lou offered. "What do you think, Ash? *Ashley?*"

Ashley scarcely heard. She was too busy staring at the couple bent toward each other in conversation beside a bright red pickup down in the parking lot. Len and Alicia. The carrot stick Ashley was munching on turned to sawdust in her mouth.

Len was leaning back against the tailgate on one elbow, his heel propped against the bumper. Alicia was wearing a white lace camisole top with her skintight jeans, and even from this distance it didn't take a telescope to see that the top three buttons were undone. The wind picked up Alicia's long hair, blowing it against Len's cheek in a soft, sinuous caress. Len smiled.

Ashley felt her insides contract into a hard knot.

It wouldn't matter to Len if I disappeared into thin air, she thought miserably. He probably wouldn't even notice.

As Ashley gazed up at Violet's portrait, a tremor of uneasiness rippled up her spine. Something was wrong. Something she couldn't quite pinpoint.

She dropped her load of schoolbooks on the coffee table and moved closer, peering up at the red-haired girl who was as familiar to Ashley now as a sister. She searched for something awry. But Violet looked as she always did, that same secret curve to her mouth, and the breathless flush to her cheeks. Violet's eyes sparkled with hidden merriment, and Ashley half-expected her to open her mouth and speak.

She found herself smiling in response, as if Violet actually had spoken to her. The knot in her stomach loosened slightly.

I've been imagining things, she decided. I'm just upset about Len. Everything is just as it should be. Violet's portrait was painted *after* her marriage, and she looks so happy. She could only look that way if she'd married the man she loved, not Mr. Calvert. Somehow, it will all work out, even if I don't go back . . .

Ashley's bubble of optimism exploded suddenly. In a flash, she saw what was wrong, what had been bothering her about the portrait. *It looks faded*, she thought. As if

115

the sun had bleached it. But the sun never shone directly on the painting.

She began to tremble. *I must be seeing things. It's just the light . . .*

But the longer she stared at it, the more convinced she became—*Violet is fading away!* Her features were slightly blurred, as if seen through an unfocused lens, and her once vivid hair was the dull color of old brick. The deep purple of her ballgown had turned a sickly pink color.

Ashley was trembling so hard she couldn't stand up any longer. She sank into the deep chintz sofa facing the fireplace, her mind spinning like a pinwheel in a windstorm.

This can mean only one thing. Violet wouldn't fade away unless . . . unless she were no longer my great-great-grandmother. If she marries Mr. Calvert, then her portrait will belong over someone else's fireplace, not mine . . .

And that would also mean—

Ashley felt the bottom of her stomach drop out. *Mom, Andy, and me. And Grandma, and Aunt Alice, and Uncle Freddy, and . . . Oh, the list was endless. We'll all disappear.*

Panic-stricken, Ashley squeezed her arms to make sure she was still all there, that she hadn't begun to disintegrate already. Her whole body was one big goosebump, as if her skin had shrunk, becoming suddenly too tight for her body. She shivered, thinking there must be a draft of cold air coming in from somewhere. Her feet and hands were blocks of ice, but her mind felt as if it were on fire with all the thoughts rushing through it.

I can't put it off any longer. I have to find a way of stopping Violet's marriage to Mr. Calvert. But how? I've already tried talking to Papa Oakes. What a disaster that was!

If only Elliot would come to Oakehurst. Maybe he and Violet could run away together. If Violet wrote to him . . . No, that wouldn't work. The letter would take too long to reach him. Maybe if she'd sent it a month before Mr. Calvert's proposal . . . but that was impossible. How could

Violet have known in advance about the mess she'd be landed in?

Suddenly, an idea popped into Ashley's head.

Of course!

Why hadn't she thought of it before?

I could send a letter to Elliot, she thought. I could say I was a friend of Violet's and that she'd asked me to write. Then I could "mail" it by computer! Violet said Elliot was at Harvard, didn't she? Well, I could set Merlin's clock to a few weeks before I made my trip to Oakehurst—that would give Elliot enough time to get to Violet before she had to marry Mr. Calvert, wouldn't it?—and just zap the letter to Harvard right from here. Ashley didn't know when Violet's wedding to Mr. Calvert was scheduled to take place, but she didn't want to take any chances.

It was wild . . . crazy . . . impossible. Ashley remembered visiting the Harvard campus on a family trip to Cambridge. Ivy-covered buildings sprawled out every which way. If the school was even half that size back in Elliot's time, she would have no way of knowing if the letter would land in the right place. Or if Elliot would ever get it.

But it just might work.

And it was the only chance Ashley had.

Chapter Twelve

"IT'S SOME KIND OF A JOKE, RIGHT? I MEAN, you don't expect me to *believe* you can actually travel back in time."

Lou lay sprawled on her stomach across Ashley's bed, propped on her elbows with her chin cupped in her hands. Her round blue eyes twinkled with laughter.

Ashley sighed. "Honestly, Lou, right now I wish it were a joke."

She'd called Lou after dinner and asked her to come over. If she didn't share this with someone soon, she'd go crazy. She'd held it inside her long enough, worrying about how to explain it without sounding as if she'd gone off the deep end already. But if her very best friend in the whole world wouldn't believe her, who would?

Lou sat up. "Oh, come on, Ash, be *serious.*"

"I'm dead serious."

Lou was quiet, as if waiting for Ashley to crack a smile or deliver a punch line.

Finally she said, "Look, Ash, I'm not saying you're nuts or anything, but you have been working awfully hard on this whatchamacallit of yours, and well, isn't it possible you sort of *imagined* the whole thing?"

Ashley jumped up and began pacing the carpet, too keyed up to sit still. "I knew you wouldn't believe me—that's why I held off telling you. But it really did happen! Cross my heart, Lou, I went back in time and I met my great-great-grandmother, Violet Beaumont. It was really weird

118

at first—oh, Lou, you can't *imagine* how weird! Then I found out that Violet was in trouble. She's in love with the man she's supposed to marry, my great-great-grandfather, but now she's being forced to marry someone else—I mean, *back then*—Oh, I don't know what I mean anymore, it's so hard to explain . . .'' She stopped her pacing, and stared at Lou, frustration welling up inside her. Now she knew how Christopher Columbus must have felt, trying to convince people the world wasn't flat.

Lou got up, and put her arm around Ashley's shoulder, gently leading her over to the bed. "I think you should lie down. Maybe you're sick. You do look a little feverish. That can cause hallucinations. Remember a couple of months ago when I had a fever of 104? I really *saw* John Lennon. He was right there in my room singing 'Imagine.' ''

Ashley pulled away. "It's not like that, Lou. I was really there!''

"Sure you were.'' Lou's mouth was pulled down with exaggerated seriousness. "Now, why don't you just lie down. Is there a thermometer around here somewhere?''

"Will you cut it out? I am not sick. I can prove it!'' Ashley ran to her closet, unzipped the garment bag in the back, and dragged out the velvet riding habit and corset she'd been wearing when she returned from Oakehurst. She held them up in front of Lou. "You see? Do these look like they came from Macy's?''

The tiniest frown of doubt crept across Lou's chubby face as she inspected the old-fashioned garments. "They could have come from the theater department. Or . . . or the Antique Boutique. What is this thing with all the laces, anyway?''

Ashley made a face. "It's a torture device they call a corset.''

Lou's eyes opened wide. "I've read about corsets . . . in books. They're supposed to squeeze you in and make you look thinner, right? Wow, where did you get it? It—it looks new.''

"It *is* new. Well, in a way it is. I was wearing it when I came back from Oakehurst—my family's plantation. But unless I can stop Violet from marrying Mr. Calvert, there won't *be* any family."

"No family? Ash, what in the world are you talking about? Last time I looked your mom was measuring the windows in the living room for new drapes, and you're right here in front of me, aren't you?" Lou reached out and gave Ashley a gentle pinch on the arm.

Ashley rubbed her arm, more reassured than annoyed by Lou's pinch. As long as she could still feel, that meant she was still all here. "Lou, you don't understand. I'm here now, but if my great-great-grandmother doesn't marry my great-great-grandfather, I won't be." She let out a frustrated sigh, sinking down on the bed. "Maybe if I start from the beginning . . ."

Ashley opened the floodgates, and all the details of her trip to Oakehurst came rushing out. As the story unfolded, Lou's expression of amused skepticism melted into one of astonished bewilderment. She's probably wondering how someone as technical-minded as I could make up something as incredible as this, Ashley thought. For one exasperated instant she had an urge to grab Lou by the straps of her overalls and shake her. Then the feeling fizzled. Look at it from Lou's point of view, she told herself. If Lou told you something as incredible as this, would you be so quick to believe it?

Lou was slowly edging toward the door. "Look, Ashley, can't we talk about this tomorrow? Maybe you'll be feeling better by then." She was clearly confused, torn between wanting to believe her best friend and her inability to accept the idea that time travel was really possible.

"Maybe I won't be around at all tomorrow," Ashley said, clutching at Lou's arm in desperation. "Lou, that's why I needed to talk to you so badly. If I can't solve Violet's problems, you might be out of a best friend."

Lou blanched. "You don't mean that, do you? I mean,

you're just kidding, aren't you? I just can't imagine . . ." Her sentence trailed off.

"You should have been here an hour ago, when I sent the letter to Elliot. Maybe that would have convinced you."

"What's the big deal about sending a letter?" Lou wanted to know.

"I sent it by computer. Back to 1861." Ashley watched Lou's round eyes grow even rounder. "I just hope he gets it. Harvard is a big place."

Lou let out a nervous giggle. "Well, that sure beats Federal Express. Going backward instead of forward."

"You can laugh all you like, but this is serious. *Dead* serious," Ashley emphasized. She slipped out of her khaki-colored jumpsuit and grabbed the corset, pulling it around her. She swiveled around so that the back of the corset, with all its dangling laces, was to Lou. "Well, if you're not going to give me any moral support, will you at least help me lace this thing up?"

Lou jumped back as if she thought the corset might bite. "What for?"

Slowly, Ashley turned to face Lou. She'd hoped her story would be enough, but clearly the only way to convince Lou was to show her. One picture, as the saying went, was worth a thousand words. But was Lou prepared for a *holographic* picture that was going to swallow her best friend? If not, she was in for quite a shock. Poor Lou! But there was no other way . . .

"I'm going back," she said gently, as if she were explaining it to a child.

"Back where?" Lou grabbed one of the laces dangling from Ashley's corset and hung on to it tightly.

She still doesn't want to believe me, but she's really afraid, Ashley thought. I guess my fear must be contagious.

"To Oakehurst," Ashley replied, her voice wobbling on the edge of panic. "And Lou, if—if for some reason I don't make it back here"—she swallowed hard, feeling panic

121

creep up her throat—"will you tell my parents what happened?"

"Tell them *what?* Ashley, what are you talking about?"

"The Civil War's going to break out any day. Back then, I mean. Even if I do get Violet and Elliot together, who knows what could happen to me. I could wind up in the middle of one of those battles Mrs. Killington is always rambling on about. Only it'll be *real,* with guns and blood . . . and . . . and people getting killed." Ashley squeezed her eyes shut, imagining herself crumpled on some battlefield. A bitter taste flooded her mouth, and for a moment she thought she might be sick. "Ashley Calhoun, born 1971, died 1861."

Ashley opened her eyes and saw a horrified look on Lou's face.

Lou backed away as far as she could go, plunking down abruptly on the window seat. "Okay, I'll go along with whatever game you're playing. But only because you're my best friend, and I owe you for all the times you stuck with me when I was acting like a weirdo." Lou tried to sound nonchalant, but her voice quavered nervously.

Suddenly, it occurred to Ashley that she might never see Lou again. Tears welled up in her eyes as she ran over and hugged Lou. "Oh, Lou, you're the best friend in the whole world. If anything happens to me, I want you to have my suede jacket and my record collection and my bike, and, oh, will you take care of Boo-Boo?"

"Hold it! I can't take much more of this!" Lou cried. Her voice grew stern. "If this is some kind of a joke, Ashley Calhoun, then you can forget about dying on some battlefield. Because I'll personally strangle you with my bare hands."

Ashley only hugged Lou tighter, tears streaming down her face. "What are best friends for?" She straightened, wiping her eyes. "Well, I'd better get going. Will you help me get dressed?"

With a groan, Lou rose and began fumbling with the laces of Ashley's corset. "Of all the crazy—"

"I'll only be gone a few minutes," Ashley interrupted before Lou got started again. "Two minutes, to be exact. For you, that is. For me, it'll be more like two days." She explained the mistake in her fractal program which had opened a tiny crack between the two times. She couldn't see Lou's face, but she could imagine its bewildered expression. "Never mind," she said with a sigh, "you'll see for yourself."

"All I know is, it better be good," Lou warned, giving the laces a hard jerk. "I don't know why, because I still don't believe in anything as crazy as time travel, but you've managed to get me really scared. I haven't been this scared since I watched *Nightmare on Elm Street.*"

There was no point in explaining any further, Ashley thought. Lou would just have to see for herself. Only this time you could call it *Nightmare at Oakehurst.*

With her corset laced, Ashley quickly tugged on the velvet skirt and jacket. It seemed to take forever, buttoning all those tiny little buttons. I'll never take zippers for granted after this, she thought.

Finally, she was ready. Now for Merlin. All she had to do was use her modem to tap into the library banks, set her computer for the right time and location, set the timer for two minutes, and activate the laser gun. Wait till Lou gets a load of this! she thought as she punched EXECUTE on her keyboard.

"You'd better step back," she warned Lou. "Or you'll end up coming with me."

Lou jumped clear of Ashley with a high, nervous laugh. "No, thanks. I didn't pack a suitcase." The battle to hang on to her skepticism was clearly growing more and more difficult.

Ashley turned her attention to the pulsing, amoebalike blob that appeared on Merlin's screen. She watched it grow off the screen, as it had before.

Ashley heard a gasp behind her, and turned to find Lou staring at her, wide-eyed, her back pressed to the door. "It's—it's some kind of light show, right?" Her voice had a ragged, hysterical edge to it. "Yeah, that's what it is, all right. I saw something like this on *That's Incredible.*"

Through the hologram wrapping itself around Ashley, Lou was only a blurry rainbow-colored shape. "It's what I've been trying to tell you all along," she called out, her voice trailing into a tinny echo. "I really found a way to travel back in time!"

A familiar tingling began in her fingertips, working its way up her arms. And—ooops!—there was that tug in her belly, like going up in an elevator.

Lou shrieked. "Ashley! Oh, my gosh, you're disappearing!"

"It's okay. I've done this before."

"Ashley, you're scaring me!" This time Lou's cry sounded very far away and muffled.

"Relax. I'll be back in no time . . . I hope." The tingling had spread through her whole body. Ashley knew it was only a matter of seconds before she would be sucked into the passageway between two times.

Faintly, through the rushing that filled her ears like long-distance telephone static, Ashley could hear Lou cry, "Wow, oh, wow, this is really heavy! Maybe *I'm* the one who's imagining things . . ."

The whirling, floating sensation stopped.

Softness. Surrounding her like a warm nest of feathers.

Blurred shapes swam into focus. Two dark polished bed-posts with knobs carved in the shape of acorns. A tall dresser reaching nearly to the ceiling. An oval looking glass in which she could just make out the watery reflection of a pale, frightened face framed with tousled red hair.

Ashley was lying on the goosedown quilt in the guest room at Oakehurst. The bed creaked as she sat up. Her head felt as if it were stuffed with cotton.

The loud ticking of a clock was the only sound she heard.

She felt heavy, numb. But not nearly as scared as the last time. She knew she could go back to her own century.

Then it struck her.

Maybe not. If my letter doesn't get to Elliot . . . and Elliot doesn't get to Violet in time, then what?

I won't be anywhere.

Clong! Clong! Clong! The deep metallic chiming of the clock seemed to vibrate in her stomach.

A sudden breeze blew in through the open window, causing the lace curtains to sigh and flutter, and scattering the carpet with a handful of purple blossoms from the wisteria vine that twisted up the side of the house.

She'd programmed Merlin to send the letter to the Harvard mail room, but she wasn't even sure that such a place existed. The letter could have landed anywhere. In a drawer or a cupboard. Under a table. Who knew if it would reach Elliot?

The skittering in her stomach got worse.

Calm down, she told herself. Violet just got engaged. The wedding won't happen overnight. There's still time.

She switched her thoughts back to Lou, imagining the expression on her face right now. Poor Lou must be going crazy! Maybe I *should* have taken her with me. But the idea of Lou here at Oakehurst was too much. Imagine Lou in a fancy gown, fluttering her eyelashes at the Southern boys. Ashley smiled. Lou would be even more of a fish out of water than I am, she thought.

The sound of a horse galloping up the drive cleared the fogginess from her brain. Clutching a bedpost for support, Ashley pulled herself upright. She was still a little dizzy. But as she stared down at her feet, a giggle popped out of her. Peeking out from under her velvet hem were her red Reebok hightops with the multicolored laces. She'd been in such a rush to get back, she'd forgotten to take them off.

Ashley crossed over to the window. Looking down on the lush, rolling lawn, she saw a man streak past on a black horse. He was bent low over the reins, and the wind whipped his gingery blond hair back from a face so red it looked as if it had been boiled. Ashley recognized him as Violet's brother, Rance, whom she had met very briefly the last time, before the ball at Fairfield. Violet had explained that Rance was seldom home now that he was training with the militia.

He was shouting something. Ashley couldn't make out his words, but from his excited expression, it sounded urgent. Then, as he drew closer, a gust of wind seemed to tear the cry from him and fling it at Ashley like a hurled stone.

"War! Papa . . . everyone . . . Mr. Lincoln's declared war!"

A cold trickle of dread ran through her. War! She'd known it was coming, but nothing could have prepared her for the terror that coursed through her now. How much longer would she be safe at Oakehurst? She had no idea. All the battles and significant dates of the Civil War were jumbled together in her head. Oh, why hadn't she paid more attention to those boring lectures of Mrs. Killington's?

What if something happens to me? Or to Violet?

Violet! Ashley leaped up. I must find her. Warn her . . . of what? Oh, this is all so confusing!

Remembering to slip off her sneakers, she shoved them under the bed and tugged on the riding boots she'd been wearing last time. They were on the floor where she'd left them, the mud caked on the soles not even dry. Then she dashed into the next room, but Violet wasn't there. She must have gone downstairs while I was sleeping, Ashley thought. Maybe to plead with her father one last time.

She picked up her skirts. Now she would have to get used to these clothes all over again. Hopping back and forth between centuries isn't like switching channels on a TV set, she thought. It's more like finding yourself in a play and realizing you don't know any of your lines.

As she made her way downstairs, Ashley could hear Papa Oakes's deep voice filtering through the closed door of his study, followed by Rance's higher voice, his words tumbling out in an excited rush. Ashley drew closer to hear

126

what they were saying. A tearful voice interrupted them. Violet!

"I won't do it, Papa! I won't marry that—that creature. I hate Wade Calvert!"

"You'll do as I say!" her father roared. Listening through the door, Ashley flinched in Violet's behalf. "The sooner the better. Your brother has just informed me that Wade's regiment will be leaving at the end of the week. Two days isn't much time to plan a wedding, I know. But we'll have to make the best of it, circumstances being what they are."

"Two days!" Violet's voice was a wail of indignation. "Oh, Papa, you can't mean it! That's—that's *gross.*"

"Gross?"

"It's a word Ashley taught me. It means barbaric."

"Exactly my point. You've been spending so much time with those Yankees, you're even beginning to sound like one yourself. The sooner you're married off to Wade Calvert, the sooner you'll stop pining for that scoundrel Elliot Beaumont."

"But, Papa—"

"Enough! The matter's settled!" Then, more softly, "Don't cry, sugar, I'm only doing what's best for you."

Ashley's heart caught in her throat. Two days! This will leave almost no time at all for Elliot to reach Violet even if he received my letter.

Suddenly the study door was flung open. Ashley had to duck quickly out of sight to avoid being caught eavesdropping.

Violet charged straight past Ashley without noticing her. Ashley tiptoed past the study door and followed her into the darkened library. Violet threw herself down on the sofa, sobbing her heart out.

Ashley rushed over and knelt beside her, feeling as if her own heart were being torn in half.

"Don't cry, Violet! We'll find a way out . . . somehow." Should she tell Violet about the letter she'd sent Elliot? No, it would be too complicated to explain. It would

127

mean telling her who she really was, and why would Violet be any easier to convince than Lou? It would only make her even more upset than she already was.

Violet lifted her tear-stained face from the cushion. "Oh, Ashley, Papa says I have to marry Mr. Calvert in *two days.*"

Ashley stroked Violet's tangled curls. "I know," she replied miserably. "I heard."

Violet collapsed back onto the cushions, sobbing. "Oh, if only Elliot were here! But he's hundreds of miles away. And he hasn't written to me in ages. I'm beginning to think he's forgotten all about me!"

"Oh, no!" Ashley cried. "I'm sure that can't be true. Maybe he *has* written, only his letter never got here."

"I don't know what to think anymore. I'm so miserable, I—I—I wish I'd never been born!"

Violet's anguished words sent an icicle of panic plunging through Ashley. If Elliot doesn't come soon, then I'll be the one who doesn't get born. Elliot, you have to come for Violet, Ashley pleaded silently. It's a matter of life and death.

Chapter Thirteen

"MY REGIMENT LEAVES IN AN HOUR, BUT I couldn't go without saying good-bye."

Brett Hathaway stood before Ashley, tall and splendid in his double-breasted gray uniform and crimson sash. His bright blue eyes seemed to pierce right through her, causing Ashley's heart to beat more quickly.

Unable to sleep the night before, she'd risen before dawn to sit in the cool air on the veranda. Lost in her thoughts, she had been startled to see Brett riding up on Beaujolais. Now she noticed that the sky had turned from milky gray to apricot, and the sun's fiery rim was peeking up over the distant red hills.

Today is Violet's wedding day, she realized with a sudden sharp pang of despair. Tonight at nine o'clock she'll become Mrs. Wade Calvert. And I'll become . . . nonexistent. Tears filled her eyes.

Brett sank down beside her on one knee, wrapping her cold fingers in his big warm hand. "Oh, Miss Beaumont, your tears tell me what I've longed to know—that you *do* care for me as I care for you."

Ashley stared at him, momentarily forgetting her despair over Violet's wedding. Is this for *real?* she wondered. Is Brett telling me he loves me?

Yes. Brett's eyes told her he did. A thousand butterflies soared up within her, fluttering and spiraling, brushing her insides with velvet wings. It was the first time a boy had ever told her he loved her, and Ashley didn't care if it *was*

129

happening a hundred years in the past or if he had misread the meaning of her tears.

Brett doesn't care if I'm klutzy, Ashley thought. He doesn't mind that I'm not beautiful.

He loves me, anyway.

She felt a mixture of astonishment and disbelief, then slowly a warm happiness flowed through her. A miracle.

But what about her feelings for Brett? It was wonderful to be loved. And yet . . .

"I—I do care about you, Brett," she replied sincerely. He had befriended her when she needed it, and she was grateful for that. But was that all?

She was so confused right now, she didn't know *what* she felt.

Brett was squeezing her hand so hard her knuckles hurt. "Then you'll wait for me? The war will be over soon, and I'll come back to you."

Ashley didn't know what to say. Somehow none of this seemed real. It was as if she'd dreamed Brett up.

"I know what you're thinking," Brett rushed on, "but let's not let politics rule our hearts. Whatever happens . . . I love you."

Ashley squirmed inwardly. How could she tell him the truth about herself?

If it wasn't so serious, it might be funny. Here was the moment she'd daydreamed about so many times—the moment a boy told her he loved her—but the boy was a hundred years older than she was!

In her daydreams she'd looked soulfully into Mr. Right's eyes, but now she looked down at the ground, tracing imaginary circles with the toe of her boot.

In her daydreams she would melt into Mr. Right's tender, warm embrace. Now she sat stiffly, her hand rigid in Brett's.

And one more thing, Ashley suddenly realized. In her daydreams Mr. Right looked an awful lot like Len Cassinerio.

In that moment she knew that she could never be in love

with Brett. Whether they came from different centuries or not.

Sure, he was handsome. And when she was around him, her mouth went dry and her pulse fluttered. But he didn't fill her thoughts when he wasn't around. Not like Len.

Maybe it was because she couldn't help feeling that Brett was infatuated with someone he'd mistaken for Leonore Beaumont, not the real her. Not Ashley Calhoun, twentieth-century time traveler.

Nevertheless, she didn't want to hurt his feelings. Poor Brett! She knew so well how it felt to be hopelessly in love with someone and not have it returned.

"I . . . I don't know what to say," she admitted honestly.

"Say yes, then."

"Yes?"

"That you'll marry me."

"Marry you! Oh, Brett, you don't understand. I can't!"

"Why not?"

"I . . . Well, for one thing, I'm only sixteen. I'm too young to get married."

"You're the same age as Violet. And she's getting married."

"To a man she doesn't love!" Ashley blurted out, then immediately regretted it.

Brett pulled his hand away from hers, his handsome face creasing with hurt. "That's it, isn't it? You don't love me. Is there someone else? A beau up North?"

Ashley thought of Len. "In a way . . . yes. Oh, Brett, I'm truly sorry. I never meant to hurt your feelings. I do like you very much. Can't we just be friends? Believe me, it's better this way. We're just too different."

"You mean because you share Mr. Lincoln's beliefs? Ashley, I don't think—"

She placed her fingertips against her lips. "That's only part of it. Oh, Brett, I don't know how to explain it. We're . . . worlds apart. Anyway, I won't be staying here much longer. I'm going home soon."

If my plan to get Violet and Elliot together works, she added to herself, nervously crossing her fingers behind her back for luck.

Brett rose stiffly, his expression sad and bewildered. "If you change your mind . . ."

An image of Len at the picnic flitted across her mind. *Yo, Ashley, if you change your mind . . .*

No, she wouldn't change her mind. Not about Brett. She belonged in the twentieth century.

Ashley rose up on tiptoe beside him and kissed his cheek gently. "Good luck, Brett." She knew his side wouldn't win the war, but she prayed he'd come out of it unharmed.

One corner of Brett's mouth twisted up in a sad little half smile. Softly he said, "Just you be careful, hear? Don't go jumping out in the road in front of anyone. I want you to be around for a while longer. No matter where you are . . ."

Ashley watched him make his way down the graveled walkway, unhitch his horse, and ride away, giving a brave, melancholy wave. His final words to her rang in her ears.

I hope to be around a while longer too, Brett, she thought silently. You'll never know how much I hope it. But it all depends on whether Elliot got my letter . . .

"Ouch!" Ashley dropped the needle and thread into her lap and brought her finger to her lips, sucking at the spot where she'd stuck herself. "It's no use, Violet, I'll never be any good at embroidery."

Violet sighed. "It doesn't matter, Ash. Teaching you was just something to get my mind away from—" She broke off, unable even to say the words.

Poor Violet! Ashley was worried about her. She was so pale. Purple smudges below her eyes gave them a hollowed look. Even her hair seemed to have lost its luster. It hung about her slumped shoulders like limp strands of crepe paper left over from a party the night before.

Ashley glanced at the clock on the mantel in Violet's

room. Six o'clock. In just a few more hours Violet Oakes would become Mrs. Wade Calvert.

She felt as dispirited as Violet. Elliot hadn't come. If he had gotten my letter, he would be here by now, she thought. Maybe Violet is right. Maybe he *did* stop caring.

Nothing made sense to Ashley anymore. There was so much she didn't understand. Once upon a time, she'd believed that history couldn't change, but here it was rearranging itself like a deck of cards being shuffled. Maybe her time jump had stirred up the wrong atoms, or upset a delicate balance somewhere in the universe.

She remembered, when she was a very little girl, reaching for a shiny red bulb that hung on the lowest branch of the Christmas tree. She'd wanted to hold that ball, keep it for her very own. But as she was pulling it off, it fell to the floor and shattered into a thousand twinkling pieces.

Ashley felt like that now. As if she had trespassed where she didn't belong. Broken something that could never be whole again.

Tears filled her eyes, but she quickly blinked them back. She had to be strong, for Violet's sake. Or at least pretend to be . . .

Ashley picked up the lace handkerchief she'd been embroidering and added the final stitches the way Violet had shown her. When it was finished, she held it up for a closer look. Not much to show for an afternoon's work—a shaky initial ''A'' surrounded by tiny blue forget-me-nots. But at least it had helped her get her mind off the thumping and scraping noises downstairs of furniture being rearranged in preparation for the wedding.

It was to be a small ceremony, not more than twenty people. Many of the men had already gone off to join their regiments, and several other families Violet knew were planning hasty weddings of their own. No one, it seemed, wanted to go to war without knowing there was someone to come home to when it was over.

For Violet, there wasn't enough time to have her own wedding dress sewn, so her mother's bridal gown had been altered to fit her. Not that Violet cared one way or another. It was clear to Ashley that a black mourning dress would have suited Violet's mood best.

Nevertheless, Violet managed to put on a brave little smile as she inspected Ashley's embroidery. "Fine work for a beginner," she declared. "But I'm curious, why did you use 'A' for Ashley instead of 'L' for Leonore, since Leonore is your real name?"

Suddenly, Ashley couldn't bear holding in the truth a moment longer. What difference did it make anymore? She'd already managed somehow to ruin Violet's whole future . . . and her own. How much worse could she make things by telling Violet who she really was?

Ashley reached over, taking Violet's delicate-boned hand in hers. Her heart thudded against her rib cage. "Violet, there's something I have to tell you . . . something about me you don't know. I'm not really who you think I am. I'm—"

She was interrupted by a thrashing noise outside. It sounded as if a tree were being shaken against the window-panes.

Violet dashed across the room to throw open the window. A large muddy boot swung over the sill, followed by a lanky figure with a shock of disheveled brown hair. Ashley stared in alarm. Who on earth—

Violet let out a startled sound that was halfway between a sob and a shriek. "Elliot!"

Chapter Fourteen

ASHLEY WAS TOO STUNNED TO MOVE. SHE SAT there, frozen in her chair, watching as Violet flew into Elliot's arms. Their two bodies seemed to become one, Violet's red curls mingling with his dark locks, their arms twined about each other so tightly it was impossible to tell them apart for a moment.

Then Violet was sobbing, and Elliot was stroking her hair, murmuring, "Hush now, my darling. I'm here. I won't ever leave you again."

"Oh, Elliot," Violet said, "Papa is forcing me to marry Mr. Cal—"

Elliot rocked her tenderly. "I know all about it. I would have come sooner, but I got the letter only last week. It was a miracle it reached me at all. It was found in the bushes outside the post room—it must have been dropped by accident when it was delivered."

Violet stared up at him with huge wet eyes. "What letter?"

Across the room, Ashley caught her breath. So her plan *had* worked . . . barely.

"The letter your friend sent on your behalf," Elliot said with a puzzled look. "Someone named Ashley. She told me what had happened, and asked me to come right away. It's a good thing I left when I did, too. Blockades are going up everywhere. I had to get off the train in Charlottesville. I took a ride with a farmer the rest of the way."

"Ashley sent you a letter? But how—" Violet turned her bewildered gaze on Ashley.

Elliot became aware of her presence and was staring at her, too. His eyes were a steady, thoughtful gray, Ashley saw. He wasn't really handsome—too thin, all knobs and knees. *Like me,* Ashley thought, suppressing a smile as she realized who she'd inherited her lanky body from.

"I'm Elliot Beaumont," he said. "Are you Ashley?"

Violet spun on him, clearly shocked. "Mercy, Elliot, don't you know your own sister?"

Those steady gray eyes continued staring at her. "My sister? I've never seen her before in my life. Leonore is in Philadelphia. She wrote to you, saying she thought it would be best if she didn't come, after all. She was frightened by all the talk of war. Don't tell me you didn't receive her letter?"

"No, I didn't," Violet said softly. Now she was staring at Ashley too, waiting for some sort of explanation.

Ashley felt as if she were shrinking, smaller and smaller. The silence in the room seemed to throb. She'd wanted Violet to know the truth, but she hadn't meant for it to come out this way.

Slowly, Ashley rose from her chair. "That's what I was trying to tell you, Violet. I'm not Leonore. I never *wanted* to be, only you all thought—" She took a deep breath, and hot air rushed into her lungs like flames. "Well, there was just no other way to explain what I was doing here, so I let you think I was Elliot's sister."

"If you're not Leonore, then who *are* you?"

Ashley felt trapped beneath Violet's bewildered gaze. But she swallowed the lump in her throat, and forced herself to speak.

"I know this is going to sound weird," she said. "But I'm—I'm your great-great-granddaughter."

Their shocked silence crashed over her like an invisible wave.

Then Violet let out a little squeak that sounded very much like a giggle. "You're my *what?*" she gasped.

"Your great-great-granddaughter. Both of yours," she added.

Elliot was frowning now. "See here, if this is your idea of some kind of joke—"

"It's not," Ashley said, feeling stronger now that the truth was out. The words came in a rush. "I wanted to tell you from the very beginning, Violet, but I didn't think you would believe me. You see, I'm from the twentieth century, but I—I found a way to travel back in time. Don't ask me how—you wouldn't understand. I'm not even sure if I understand, myself . . . except that I'm here, and that's what counts, isn't it? I even found out how to get back. It's sort of complicated, but the way it works is—" She stopped when she realized that Violet and Elliot were eyeing her as if she'd suddenly sprouted two heads and a pair of wings. She sighed. "You don't believe a word I'm saying, do you?"

One emotion after another flitted across Violet's face—affection, loyalty, puzzlement, and finally, disbelief. She looked the way Lou had when Ashley let her in on the time-traveling secret. Only this time, Ashley realized, I can't prove I'm telling the truth. Not yet. Without direct control of Merlin, I'll have to wait until the fractal completes itself before they can watch me disappear into another time. And that will take . . . let's see, another couple of hours.

Finally Violet spoke. "It's . . . it's not that I don't trust you, Ash. I believe *you* believe what you're saying. But . . . well, you have to admit it's pretty farfetched."

"It certainly is." Elliot was eyeing her with suspicion now. "When I received your letter, I imagined I should be grateful to you, but how do you expect me to trust someone who tells such tall tales?" He turned to Violet, frowning. "What if this is a trick? Your loyalty to the Confederacy is suspect, no doubt. Not to mention mine. This girl could be a spy. She could have lured me here only to turn me in."

Ashley was silent. How could she prove he was wrong? How could she prove anything?

But Violet only shook her head. "No, Elliot, I don't

137

believe Ashley is a spy. I haven't known her long, and it's true, I don't know much about her. But I'd trust her with my life. Don't ask me why, just instinct, I guess."

"Thank you, Violet," Ashley said, tears of gratitude filling her eyes.

Violet smiled. "Well, I've always suspected there was something mighty strange about you, Ash."

Ashley struggled for some way to convince them. "I wish I could find some way to show you what it's like where I come from. It's so different. We have things you don't have, like . . . well, like cars—that's a buggy without a horse, they're powered by machines, and go very fast. And we have movies—pictures on a big screen that tell a story—and television, that's like movies, only a box picks up transmissions from the air . . . and computers like the one that got me here . . ."

Violet sank into the nearest chair as if she were on the verge of fainting. "Computers?" she echoed weakly, obviously not having the slightest idea what Ashley was babbling about.

"A computer is—well, to put it simply, it's a machine that computes. It can add numbers and work out problems that would take our brains hours to find the answers for. Like Merlin—that's my computer. Merlin brought me here."

Elliot stood there, shaking his head. "If you're making this all up, I must admit you have quite an imagination. Machines that add numbers! Horseless buggies!" His stern expression gave way and he began to chuckle. "Next you'll be telling me there's such a thing as wagons that fly!"

"In a way," Ashley said. "They're called airplanes. You can get in an airplane and be flown anywhere in the world."

"Land sakes!" squeaked Violet. "That *is* hard to believe!"

Ashley realized she may have said too much. After all, how could she possibly expect them to imagine all those things she took so much for granted? Seeing it from their point of view, the idea of a flying wagon was pretty ludicrous.

"Listen, I know it sounds crazy, and maybe I never will be able to convince you that I'm telling the truth, but where I come from is not really what's important right now. What *is* important is getting the two of you away from Oakehurst before anyone finds out that Elliot is here."

A trace of suspicion still lingered in Elliot's eyes. "If Violet trusts you, perhaps that should be good enough for me." He bit his lip. He draped one arm protectively around Violet's shoulders. "But if something should go wrong, I could never forgive myself."

"Elliot, if this was a trick, do you think I would have bothered with a story about myself that sounds so unbelievable?"

Elliot thought for a moment, and Ashley could see the last bit of distrust melting from his face. "I suppose not. No, a spy would be much more, well, discreet."

Ashley smiled. Elliot may still think I'm crazy, she reflected, but at least he knows I'm on their side. Now we can get on with their plan to run away.

Suddenly, she realized what all this meant. Things might very well turn out the way they were supposed to. Relief washed through her. I just might get born, after all! she thought.

But they weren't out of the woods yet. "Elliot," she asked, "can you get back the way you came, or will the roads be blocked?"

"I believe we can get through," he said, his gray eyes thoughtful. "The troops aren't really organized yet. In a few days perhaps they will be. But it still won't be easy, especially if Violet's father decides to come after us."

Violet's hand flew to her mouth, her eyes growing wide with alarm. "Papa! He's right, Ash. Papa will chase us . . . drag me back."

"Unless he doesn't know you're gone," Ashley mused aloud, an idea forming in her mind. Crazy . . . but it just might work. "How much time would you need?" she asked.

Elliot was silent for a moment, considering the problem. "A couple of hours," he said. "Long enough to get to the train depot in Charlottesville, where no one would recognize us. They may ask questions, but I can pretend to be an enlisted man. I'll say I'm taking my wife to live with my mother while I'm off fighting for the cause." He touched Violet's cheek. "It's true, in a way. I *will* be fighting, but not for the side they think. You'll stay with my aunt and the *real* Leonore in Philadelphia, my dearest."

Ashley saw the bereft look on Violet's face. Poor Violet. She's thinking about all she'll be leaving behind. Her home. Her family and friends. Her whole way of life.

A little crimp of fear worked its way into Ashley's stomach. Suppose Violet doesn't love Elliot enough to give up all that?

But Ashley had underestimated Violet. She wasn't the helpless, fluttering belle she often pretended to be. Sad but dry-eyed, her gaze swept the room, as if she were silently saying her good-byes. When she turned to Elliot, her face was radiant with love and determination.

"Philadelphia won't seem far," she said, adding with a little smile. "Besides, I think my heart already went North some time ago." Then her forehead wrinkled in a frown of uncertainty. "But however will we get to Charlottesville without Papa catching up with us? The wedding's so soon, they're certain to find out I'm missing almost immediately."

Now it was time for Ashley to reveal her plan.

"They won't have to know," she said, swallowing hard against the knot of nervousness in her throat. "I've been thinking . . . suppose I pretend to be you. I'm only a little taller than you are, Violet. And we have the same color hair. With your bridal veil over my face, well, maybe I could pull it off . . . for a little while at least. And that's all the time you'll need."

Violet stared at her as if deciding that Ashley really *was* crazy; then abruptly she laughed. "Well, it's the wildest notion you've come up with yet, but it just might work, Ashley Whoeveryouare."

Ashley helped Violet pack a few things she would need for the journey in a small carpetbag. Then she remembered the Reeboks she'd left under her bed in the other room and ran in to get them for Violet.

"Wear these," she said. "You'll be needing them more than I will. Climbing down the trellis can be dangerous."

Violet stared at the gym shoes for a moment, as if they might bite her. "Land sakes!" she cried. "What are they?"

"They're sports shoes. Back home, we wear them to jog in."

"Jog?"

"Oh, never mind. It's too complicated to explain, and you probably wouldn't believe me, anyway. Here, sit down, and I'll put them on you."

Violet allowed Ashley to lace her feet into the shoes. When she stood up, a grin spread across her face. "I don't know where they come from—and maybe I don't *want* to know—but they make more sense than the silly shoes I've been wearing all my life!"

Ashley suppressed a laugh. The picture of Violet in her ruffled full-skirted gown, wearing Reeboks, was too funny for words.

"Just take good care of them," Ashley said. "It'll be another century before you can buy a new pair."

Elliot beckoned to Violet from the window. "We'd best hurry," he said in a lowered voice. "It'll take longer to get there, with you riding sidesaddle."

Violet exchanged a conspiratorial glance with Ashley, then looked over at him, her brows arching. "Who said anything about sidesaddle?"

"I thought . . ."

"Well, things are different now." Violet turned back to Ashley, hugging her tightly, and murmured, "No matter who you really are, I have so much to thank you for, Ash. I don't even know where to begin."

141

"You don't have to," Ashley said. "Let's just say it's all in the family."

"I wish we didn't have to say good-bye. Will I ever see you again?"

At moments like this, Ashley imagined there was something like a keepsake chest in her mind, a place to store memories such as these where they would never get old and faded. In it she would put this, so she would remember it always: the warmth of Violet's embrace, the sweet smell of her lavender perfume, the friendship they shared—a friendship that had bridged two centuries.

"I don't think so," Ashley replied, tears gathering in her eyes. "But I won't forget you, Violet." She thought of Violet's portrait hanging over the fireplace." I couldn't, even if I wanted to."

Violet sniffed. "I won't forget you, either." A tear rolled down her cheek.

Ashley reached for the handkerchief she'd embroidered, which lay atop the sewing basket, and handed it to Violet.

"I should be crying, instead," she said. "I'm the one who's going to be stuck marrying Mr. Calvert!"

Violet's eyes widened in horror above the lace fringe of the handkerchief, which she was using to mop her cheeks with. "Oh, Ashley, I didn't think. I mean . . . will you really have to go through with it?"

"I hope not. I'll stall as long as I can."

"But when they find out you're not me . . . oh, Ash, Papa will be so angry! And the Lord only knows what Mr. Calvert will do. I've heard tell he *beats* his slaves . . ."

Ashley tried not to think that far ahead. "Don't worry, Violet. If I'm lucky, I'll be home before then."

"Home?" Violet smiled. "Oh, you mean in the future."

Ashley drew back, surprised. "I thought you didn't believe me!"

"I'm not sure I do, but—"Violet looked down at her feet in their Reeboks— "there is something mighty odd about all this, and I'm not sure how else to explain it."

Ashley followed Violet's gaze. "Just think of them as UFOs."

"As *what?*"

"Unidentified Future Objects." She picked up Violet's carpetbag and carried it over to the window, where Elliot was waiting.

"Good-bye, Elliot." Ashley extended her hand. "And good luck."

"Good-bye, mysterious lady." Elliot held her hand in both of his. "I suppose I do owe you more than just a thank you, after all."

"Being born is more than thanks enough," Ashley said. Then she turned to Violet and hugged her one last time. "Whether you really think I'm from the future or not, you know you can think of me as a friend . . . no matter what century we're in." Tears welled up in the corners of her eyes.

"I'll let you know when we make it to Philadelphia," Violet whispered. "I don't know how yet. But I'll find a way . . ."

Somehow Ashley had a feeling she would.

Chapter Fifteen

THERE WAS A SOFT KNOCK ON THE DOOR. "MIZ Violet? Your pa wants to know when you're goin' to be ready. Everybody's waitin' in the parlor."

Panic rose thickly in Ashley's throat. Her stomach quivered. In a voice as close to Violet's honeyed drawl as she could imitate, she called through the locked door, "Just a minute more . . ."

"That's what you said the last time." The door handle rattled. "Why don't you let me in so I can help you?"

"I—I don't need any help, Mince. Please, just tell my—my father I'll be down soon."

"You don't sound like yourself, Miz Violet. Are you feelin' poorly?"

Ashley coughed. "No, I'm . . . fine." She only hoped Mince couldn't hear the thundering of her heart through the door. To her own ears it sounded like a jackhammer breaking up a sidewalk.

What if I really have to go through with this? she wondered, sagging against the door frame as the sound of Mince's footsteps receded down the hallway. What if I really have to *marry* Mr. Calvert?

The thought made her stomach flop heavily onto its side, as if she'd just eaten a whole tub of french fries.

For the dozenth time, she glanced at the pretty little gilt clock on the mantel, willing the hands to move. But it read only ten minutes after eight. Two minutes later than the last time she'd looked. If her calculations were correct, she wasn't due to be zapped back to Westdale for twenty more minutes. Could she stall that long?

There was Violet and Elliot to consider, too. She thought of them riding along the dark roads to Charlottesville. If all went well, they would be nearing the train depot by now. Every minute she stalled would only bring them that much closer . . .

Ashley dashed to the mirror. Can I fool them into thinking I'm Violet? she wondered.

The reflection in the wavy glass reassured her. Instead of a gawky ugly duckling, she saw a swan. In the ivory silk wedding dress that had belonged to Violet's mother, Ashley seemed to float and shimmer, like a princess in a fairy tale. She smoothed her hand over the billowing cloud of her skirt, and straightened the froth of lace spilling down the snugly fitting bodice. She'd even gotten her hair to behave for a change. Tucked up under Violet's hairpiece in back, with a few finger-curled ringlets in front, it didn't look half-bad, she thought.

Ashley gently lifted the veil that was draped across the back of the chair beside her. It was made of yards and yards of the finest gauzelike lace fastened to a crown made of tiny seed pearls. Very carefully, she fitted the crown over her head, letting the veil cascade about her shoulders like a waterfall.

What if Len could see me now? she wondered. Would he think I was pretty? As pretty as Alicia? Would he ask me to the Homecoming Dance?

She closed her eyes, imagining that the filmy veil brushing her cheek was Len's hand holding the flame-colored leaf to her hair. Soon she would be back in Westdale. Soon she would see Len . . .

A knock on the door. Louder this time. Crack! Crack! Ashley's heart jumped.

"Violet! I've had just about enough of your nonsense. Now, are you coming out of there, or do I have to break this door down?" Papa Oakes's stern voice exploded through the door.

Ashley shrank to the farthest corner of the room. Making her voice very small, she called, "Coming, Papa."

His voice became sugary, pleading. "Violet, honey, I know you're nervous and all, but the preacher's waiting. And Wade's getting very anxious. Now I know you didn't have your heart set on marrying him, but I'm sure once you get to know each other better . . . Violet?"

"Yes, Papa?" Ashley could feel her heart beating in her neck, her ears. Her stomach flopped over once again.

"Open this confounded door! NOW!"

It was no use. She couldn't stall any longer. She would have to go downstairs and face the music. The wedding march, to be exact.

Ashley lowered the gauzy layers of veil over her face, satisfied to see that her features were only a blur behind it. Now, if she could only manage to get downstairs without tripping . . .

She forced her legs to move, to carry her across the room. Each movement felt as if she were rolling a boulder in front of her. She grasped the door handle, which felt like a lump of ice against her sweaty palm, remembering to hunch down a little to make herself look shorter.

Staring into Papa Oakes's thunderous face, Ashley was glad for the veil, which not only hid her face from view but softened everything before her to a misty blur. The dark gleam of his eyes was the only thing that penetrated the layers of lace in front of her eyes.

He cleared his throat with a sound that rumbled low in his chest. "Well, now, you're a pretty sight, aren't you? I only wish your mother were alive to see you." His voice had gone soft with affection, and Ashley realized he really did care about Violet, in his own stern way, in spite of all his shouting.

She took the arm he offered, hoping he couldn't hear the wild thumping of her heart. Slowly they made their way to the stairs. At the landing, Ashley paused to say a silent prayer.

Please, Merlin, please take me home. I don't want to

146

*marry Mr. Calvert. Who knows what terrible things he'll
do to me when he finds out I'm a fake? Oh, please* . . .

As if to taunt her, the soft strains of the wedding march
being played on the piano in the parlor drifted up the stairs.
Da-dum-de-dum. Da-dum-de-dum . . .

Ashley's legs had become the consistency of warm
Jell-O. She wasn't sure she'd make it downstairs without
her knees collapsing. She clung more tightly to Papa
Oakes's steady arm as they descended one step at a time.

Please, Merlin . . .

The wedding march became louder, seemed to pound in
her veins. She smelled something sweet. Flowers. A murmur of voices could be heard over the music as they approached the parlor.

A misty blur of faces all turned toward her at once as
she glided into the parlor. And in the center of all the
flowers and faces, like a hard black stone, stood Wade
Calvert. His face was a blur. All she could see was his
black beard and the black suit he wore.

The music stopped. And suddenly she was alone, standing beside Wade, her heart banging like crazy inside the
hollow drum of her chest.

The preacher began to speak. "We are gathered here
together in the presence of . . ." She could barely distin-
guish the words. They seemed to rain down on her in one
long cold meaningless drizzle. Beside her, she could feel
Wade Calvert's oily presence. She could *smell* him. He
smelled like a furnace. Then he said something in his oily
voice that made her jump.

"I do."

The preacher turned to Ashley. "Do you, Violet Oakes,
take this man to be your lawful wedded husband, to have
and to hold, in sickness and in health, till death do you
part?"

Ashley instinctively shrank back. No! her mind
screamed. It was like being trapped in a nightmare and not
being able to wake up.

Hushed silence. Everyone waiting for her to say *I do.*

147

She opened her mouth, but no words came out.

A bubble rose up her throat, exploding in a hiccup.

Feet shuffled, chairs creaked. There were a few embarrassed snickers. She hiccupped again into the silence.

Now the black hulk that was Wade came even closer to her, looming over her like a creature rising out of the fog in a horror movie. The voices became a confused buzzing. Someone was squeezing her arm. Hard.

"Violet!" a gruff voice hissed.

"No!" She choked. "No . . . I can't marry you!"

The hand squeezed harder.

At first, Ashley thought the tingling in her fingers was a result of Wade squeezing her arm. Then the tingling spread through her whole body. No, it wasn't Wade. It was—

Merlin! Oh, thank goodness . . .

Ashley nearly cried out with relief when she looked down at her hands and saw that they had become transparent.

A wave of shocked cries washed over the room. Wade seemed to be receding . . . becoming a grayish blur . . .

A woman screamed. A high, piercing noise that sounded very far away. There was a clattering sound as if a chair had been knocked over.

"She's a ghost!" someone else yelled.

Ashley didn't care. She was already being swept away . . . back to where she belonged . . . back to her own time . . .

Chapter Sixteen

SOMEONE WAS HUGGING HER. HARD.

A blurry Lou swam into focus.

Ashley saw that Lou was crying, tears running down her round cheeks and plopping from her chin onto the bib of her overalls.

"I was so freaked out. I didn't know if you were coming back!" Lou cried. "Oh, Ashley, did you . . . is it really *true?* . . . Did you really find a way to go back in time?" Lou stepped back, looking at Ashley, her round blue eyes growing even rounder. "Ashley! What on earth are you doing in that dress? You look like . . . like . . ."

"Like a bride? Well, I almost was."

Ashley laughed—a laugh that seemed to have been scooped up from the very deepest part of her. In one long whoosh, all the knots in her stomach came untied. She was so glad to be home. And everything was going to be all right. Elliot and Violet were together. And neither she nor her great-great-grandmother had been forced to marry Mr. Calvert.

"I don't believe it," Lou said, wiping at her tears. "I thought I was ready for the space brigade. I mean I was really blown away. And you're *laughing.*"

Ashley pushed her veil from her face, and spun across the room, arms outspread, her white lace skirts floating out from her ankles. "Oh, Lou, it's such a long, complicated story. I don't know where to begin!" She collapsed backward onto her bed. Still dizzy from the effects of time traveling, she watched the ceiling spin in slow circles.

"Try the beginning." Lou wasn't crying anymore. Her moon face was sober as she sat down next to Ashley, crossing her legs on the quilt. "I'm ready to listen now."

An hour, a huge bowl of popcorn, and two steaming mugs of hot chocolate later, Ashley had told Lou the entire story from beginning to end. Her throat was hoarse from talking so much.

"Whew!" Lou blew out her cheeks, which were flushed with excitement. Her eyes were huge, as if she'd seen a ghost or a werewolf. "Do you know what this *means*, Ash?"

"Yeah. It means my whole family won't get wiped out of existence, after all. And I'll be sticking around the twentieth century for a while." Ashley brushed popcorn crumbs from her lap. She had changed back into her jeans and a baggy boat-necked cotton sweater. She wiggled her toes, enjoying the delicious comfortableness of the Chinese slippers she'd exchanged for Violet's hard, pointy boots. She stretched her legs across the window seat.

Lou sat cross-legged facing Ashley on the carpet beside the bed, her head resting against the mattress, the empty popcorn bowl nestled between her knees. The overhead light glinted off the "No Nukes" button pinned to her bib, and there was a smear of chocolate curving up like an apostrophe from one corner of her mouth.

"That's not what I meant," Lou said, "though of course I'm delighted my best friend isn't floating around out there somewhere, orbiting Saturn."

"It's not like that," Ashley said, giggling. "Honestly, you should try it. Wait a minute, I take that back. Maybe you shouldn't. Once you start messing around with the past, you never know what you're going to find."

Lou shivered. "I think I'll pass for now. I'm not ready for the Twilight Zone. At least not yet." She fished around in the bowl for the last bits of popcorn, poking an unpopped kernel in her mouth and crunching down on it with a hard, tooth-cracking sound. "What about you? Are you sorry you went?"

Ashley thought about it. Was she sorry? No. Not now, looking back. "It's sort of like riding a roller coaster," she told Lou. "You don't realize how much fun it is until you're getting off."

"Oh, Ashley, do you realize what you've done? I mean, what's going to happen when people find out about this? You'll be in *The National Inquirer!* You'll be world famous! They'll probably give you the Nobel Prize, or elect you President or something."

Ashley shook her head, then said quietly, "No one is going to find out."

"Do you really think you can keep something this big a secret?"

"Look." Ashley leaned forward. "So far, the only two people in the entire world who know about it are you and me. Besides, no one would believe it if I told them. *You* didn't at first. That's one of the benefits of being a kid— you can get away with all kinds of things and people think, 'Oh, she couldn't possibly have done *that,* she's just a kid.' "

Lou smiled. "I know what you mean. Who would have thought a sixteen-year-old kid could unravel one of the great mysteries of all time?"

"My dad was only nineteen when he built his first computer."

"Yeah. And my parents were reading *The Wall Street Journal* when everybody else their age was rocking out to Fresh Cream and the Grateful Dead."

They were both silent.

Then Lou shook her head and said softly, "Wow. I still don't believe it. You really did it. You really found a way to travel back in time."

"It's funny," Ashley said, "back there at Oakehurst I didn't really exist, theoretically that is, but I found out a lot about myself, anyway."

"Like what?" Lou put the popcorn bowl aside and leaned forward, hugging her knees to her chest.

"Like I'm not as klutzy as I thought I was. I mean, I'm

151

not exactly Princess Di, either. But that's okay. I'm sick of pretending to be someone else. I don't want to be Alicia Sanchez, or Leonore Beaumont, or my mother. After all that pretending back there, I just want to be myself.''

Lou grinned. ''I could have told you that. And saved you all the trouble you went through.''

''I think I had to find out for myself.''

''Was it so hard—being a Southern belle?''

''Well, it was hard to breathe, for one thing. You don't know what torture is until you've worn a corset. And those dresses.'' She rolled her eyes. ''Now I know where the person who invented parachutes got the idea. But''—she thought about Brett, and smiled—''in some ways it wasn't so bad.''

Lou got up, her kneecaps making little popping sounds. She squeezed in next to Ashley on the window seat, looping an arm about her shoulders. ''I'm glad about one thing,'' she said.

''What?''

''That you decided not to stay in the past.''

Ashley let out a weary sigh that seemed to encompass the entire room. I'm really okay, she thought. I did so many things I never thought I could do. I learned how to flirt, and how to dance. And I took risks, too. I faced up to Papa Oakes. I told Violet and Elliot the truth. And I almost wound up married to Wade Calvert!

But now I'm home.

And this is where I belong.

She leaned her head against Lou's plump shoulder. ''Me, too.''

''What do you think of this one?'' Eugenie Calhoun held a scrap of flowered wallpaper against a square of plum-colored carpet.

Books of carpet samples and snippets of wallpaper and fabric were spread across the dining room table. Ashley sighed. Here we go again. Mom's got redecorating fever. I wonder what part of the house will be under attack next.

152

Ashley pointed to a carpet sample the same dusky shade of pink as the skirt her mother was wearing. "Antique Rose," the fine print underneath said. "I like that one. Which room is it for?"

Eugenie rubbed her thumb across the Antique Rose plush. "Oh, it's not for us. I'm doing a couple of rooms for the Jordans down the street." She looked up at Ashley, her delicate face lit with a shy smile of triumph.

"Mom, you're kidding! When did this happen?"

"Last week. Vivian Jordan stopped by for coffee. It's been a while since she's seen the house, and she just couldn't get over what I'd done with the front room and the den. She asked me if I'd consider doing some decorating for her. So I guess you could say I'm in business. Part-time, anyway."

Ashley stared at her mother. It was so perfect. Mom was a genius when it came to decorating, choosing the exact shade of curtain to go with the wallpaper and the couch, finding unusual lamps and knickknacks in out-of-the-way specialty shops. And the result was always homey and inviting.

"That's great, Mom. I always thought you were wasting your talents, using them only on us," Ashley told her.

Eugenie flashed her a grateful smile. "I always wanted to go into business. I just wasn't sure I was good enough. You and Dad . . . you're the brains in the family. I suppose I've always been a bit jealous of you."

"Of me?" Ashley was shocked. "That's weird, Mom. Because I've always been jealous of *you*. I mean, you're so graceful and everything. And you always know the right thing to say to people when you meet them."

"Is *that* why you've been so preoccupied lately?" Eugenie peered at her with concern. "Oh, honey, I worry about you sometimes . . . spending all that time alone in your room with your computer."

"Don't worry about me, Mom." Ashley tried to keep a straight face. "I never get lonely as long as I have Merlin."

"Amazing. What they do with computers these days."

"Amazing," Ashley agreed.

Eugenie's gaze wandered back to the cluttered table. She picked up a swatch of loosely woven drapery fabric. "I think this will look just perfect on Vivian's big picture window. It'll pick up the highlights in the rug."

Ashley sank down in the chair next to her mother's. "Mom? Can I talk to you about something?"

"Mmmm . . ."

"It's for school," Ashley fibbed. "We're supposed to do our family tree as an assignment for history. And I was wondering . . . uh, well . . . if you knew what happened to my great-great-grandmother Violet after the Civil War."

Eugenie leaned back in her chair, her drapery samples momentarily forgotten, a faraway look in her eyes. "Haven't I told you the story? I'm sure I must have. Well, Violet and her husband—that would be your great-great-grandfather, Elliot Beaumont—they returned to the South after the war. To Oakehurst."

"To Oakehurst? But I thought all those old plantations were destroyed during the war. You know, like Tara in *Gone with the Wind.*"

"Most were. It was a miracle that Oakehurst survived. But I think that must have had something to do with the legend."

"Legend?" Ashley's heart began to race.

"Mmm. Oakehurst was said to be haunted by a spirit which had taken on the form of Violet Oakes. It was even said to have driven one gentleman mad—one of Violet's suitors, who claimed he married the spirit, fooled into thinking it was Violet. They say he was never the same afterward. I guess the Yankees must have been superstitious too, because they stayed away for the most part."

"So Violet and Elliot moved back to Oakehurst? That's wonderful! They're going to be so hap—I mean, I'm sure they *were* very happy about that." Ashley realized she was going to have to be a lot more careful about what she said.

But Eugenie didn't appear to have noticed her slipup.

154

"It's a funny thing," she mused, "but I remember my grandmother telling me that people thought Violet was a bit odd herself. Quite often she'd say the strangest things . . . or know something was going to happen before it happened. And she became the talk of the countryside when she took up riding astride her horse, just like a man. Of course, everybody thought it was because of the years she'd spent up North during the War . . .''

Ashley just smiled to herself.

"I know what you're thinking." Ashley spoke in a whisper to Violet's portrait. "That's where you got that Mona Lisa smile of yours. *I'm* your secret. And for over a hundred years you've been waiting for me to figure it out." The realization was so powerful, Ashley felt shaken by it, as if a strong wind had picked her up in the air and dropped her back down again.

Violet didn't answer. From her place over the mantel, she just went on smiling that secret, knowing smile of hers.

The vividness of the portrait was back, Ashley was reassured to notice. The purple blue of Violet's gown seemed to leap out at her. Her features were alive, those merry amber eyes actually dancing. Ashley felt that if she could reach up and touch the hand that rested in those amethyst folds, it would be warm.

Ashley stared at the hand. There was something about it. Something she hadn't noticed before.

Then it struck her.

It wasn't Violet's hand. It was the handkerchief held delicately between two fingers. Just a scrap of lace—not something you would pay attention to, Ashley thought. Unless . . .

It can't be, she thought. I'm imagining things.

She pushed a chair in front of the fireplace, and stood up on it for a closer look, her heart pounding with excitement.

There. Almost invisible unless you looked closely, and knew what it was.

155

A tiny "A" amateurishly embroidered in one corner, surrounded by forget-me-nots.

The handkerchief blurred out of focus as tears filled Ashley's eyes. "Oh, Violet, you promised to get a message to me, and you did. You remembered . . ."

Chapter Seventeen

ASHLEY WATCHED LEN AND ALICIA OUT OF THE corner of her eye as they stood at the far end of her locker row. She winced in pain as Alicia dipped a scarlet-nailed hand into his locker, withdrawing a hot pink chiffon hair ribbon from its jumbled depths, like a magician pulling a scarf from a hat. Well, Alicia certainly seemed to have worked her spell on Len, Ashley thought. Was she planning on taking over his whole life?

Only the hem of Alicia's microscopic leather miniskirt peeked out from under her oversize rhinestone-studded sweatshirt. She bent close to Len. Then with a pearl of silvery laughter, she knotted the hot pink scarf about his muscular arm. Len shook his head, giving her a disgusted look, but he didn't remove the scarf, Ashley observed with a pang. As he sauntered past her on his way to his next class, Alicia fastened to one arm and the bright bow to the other, Ashley quickly ducked her head into her locker, pretending to be madly searching for something so he wouldn't see the tears in her eyes.

Give up, Ashley Calhoun, she told herself. You'll never have more than the back of Len's head during history. Especially now that Alicia's on the scene. How do you expect to compete with that boa constrictor? She's obviously got herself so wrapped around Len's life it would probably take the entire Dallas Cowgirls cheerleader squad to get his attention away from her for even one second.

Going back to her great-great-grandmother's time had changed certain things about her life, but she would never be able to make herself over into another Alicia. Nor did she want to.

But Ashley couldn't get her mind off Len, no matter how hard she tried. The more she attempted to forget about Len, the more he kept popping up in her thoughts. Tromping through a pile of fallen leaves on her way to the annex for Spanish class, she relived the moment when Len had held that scarlet leaf to her hair, his knuckles brushing her cheek. Her whole face glowed with the warmth of the memory.

It's useless, she decided. Trying to forget about Len is like not thinking about elephants.

"Hi, Red!" Pint-sized Tina Scott paused to greet Ashley as she was strolling past with Charmaine Parker. "Hey, I just came from Mrs. Killjoy's class," she said, referring to nobody's favorite history teacher. "She popped a surprise Civil War quiz on us last period. I have a feeling you might be in for the same treatment. Hope you studied." Tina's petite frame was swallowed up by an oversize striped dress that made her look as if the next strong wind might carry her off.

Ashley couldn't keep from smiling just a little. What would Tina say if I told her I'd done one better—I was actually *there?*

"Oh, I'll manage," she told Tina. "But thanks for the warning."

Charmaine's perpetually dreamy expression turned suddenly mournful. "I just know I flunked it. My morning horoscope said I would be caught off guard by an unwelcome surprise today. I guess this just isn't a lucky day for Libras."

Ashley and Tina exchanged here-she-goes-again looks. Charmaine was into everything from astrology to astral projection and had even dabbled in white witchcraft. Moon Maiden, that's what Tina affectionately called her. And she certainly looked the part in the antique linen nightgown she

158

wore as a dress, belted at the waist with a tooled leather belt, with her curly chestnut hair tucked under a wide-brimmed straw hat.

Charmaine is probably the only one of my friends who wouldn't laugh if I told her I'd gone back in time, Ashley thought. Maybe I should give *her* ideas a fair chance.

On impulse, she asked, "Do you remember what the horoscope said was in store for Capricorns today?"

Charmaine's forehead crinkled under the floppy brim of her hat. "Well, I don't usually read them all. But as it so happens, my mom's a Capricorn. We read ours aloud to each other over breakfast. Let's see . . . Oh, yeah, I remember now." A broad smile lit her dreamy doe-eyed face. " 'Look ahead to the future. Don't dwell on the past. Unexpected opportunities may come your way.' "

Ashley smiled. In her case, it should have read, "Don't dwell *in* the past." As far as unexpected opportunities went, well . . . that remained to be seen. Right now she wasn't holding out too much hope for opportunities in the romance department.

"Thanks," she told Charmaine, "but if I don't dwell on the past, I won't pass Mrs. K.'s test."

The second bell jangled, and they all hurried off to their classes. Spanish was in the new annex wing behind the original red-brick ivy-covered building, which had been donated to the town by an eccentric millionaire named Lloyd Hanshaw eighty years ago. Ashley could hear Mr. Ortega practicing one of his tenor arias as she jogged down the hallway, neatly sidestepping a janitor's pushbroom that had fallen across her path. *Way to go, Calhoun,* she congratulated herself. Only a few days ago, she would have tripped over that for sure!

She scooted into her seat just as the final bell pealed. Roly-poly Mr. Ortega, the Pavarotti of O. Henry High, was just finishing his aria from the opera *Rigoletto*. Ashley planted her elbows on her desk, and settled her chin on her upturned palms to enjoy the rest of the show. Mr. Ortega was not only teaching them Spanish but also making music lovers of his students. That was the great thing about O. Henry. For every teacher like Mrs. Killington, there were three or four like Mr. Ortega.

Across the aisle from Ashley sat Jordan Zimmerman. Last year she'd had a crush on him, but had given up after a while, knowing it was useless. Despite the fact that Jordan still had "railroad tracks" on his teeth, he was one of the cutest, most popular boys on campus.

Now she noticed that Jordan was looking over at her with more than friendly interest. Was it just her imagination? Had she really changed that much? A new thought flew into her head. Maybe Jordan had looked at her this way before, but she just hadn't allowed herself to believe he could be interested.

She remembered now how Bif O'Neill had acted toward her at the picnic. And of course there was Brett . . .

Maybe I'm not so hopeless, she thought. And maybe I just have to prove it to Len. Besides, what do I have to lose, anyway? If I don't make a move, then I'll definitely end up with zero. If I do, then at least I'll have some chance, even if it's a tiny one.

"Señorita Calhoun, you like *Rigoletto?*" Mr. Ortega's voice boomed across the classroom.

Flustered, Ashley looked up. "Huh?"

Mr. Ortega grinned, both chins bobbing. "You looked as if you were enjoying the music. But perhaps you were simply off in another world?"

Several students tittered. Ashley could feel herself redden. Then she realized Mr. Ortega couldn't really see through her and read her thoughts; he was just teasing her.

She smiled. "Sing something else, Mr. Ortega."

The whole class applauded, calling out, "Encore! Encore!"

Later, as she sat in history, Ashley felt her optimistic mood begin to sag. Staring at the back of Len's head, she was full of her old uncertainty. It wasn't true that she had nothing to lose by letting Len know how she felt about him. She could lose her pride, wind up making a complete fool of herself . . .

Len might laugh at her. And if he did that, she would die.

Die!

She chewed on the eraser end of her pencil as Mrs. Killington passed around mimeographed pages to the class. The pop quiz Tina had warned her about. Ashley sniffed the purple and white sheets, then looked over the questions. They were all about the Civil War.

One question in particular seemed to jump out at her:

Uncle Tom's Cabin, by Harriet Beecher Stowe, caused outrage against slavery in the North, but the South remained indifferent. True or False.

Ashley circled False, even though she suspected Mrs. Killington would mark it wrong. She just couldn't bring herself to betray Violet. It had taken great courage for Violet to go against everything her father had believed in.

It occurred to Ashley that if she had even one iota of Violet's courage, she would show Len how much she cared about him. Violet had sacrificed everything for Elliot. All Ashley was risking was a little pride. Okay, a lot of pride. But it was time to show Violet that some of her courage had been passed on to her great-great-granddaughter.

Before she could change her mind, Ashley tore the corner off a piece of loose-leaf paper and scribbled hastily: "I changed my mind. Meet me after school at the baseball diamond. Ashley."

Gathering all the courage she possessed in one fiery burst of determination, she folded the note into a tiny square and tossed it over his shoulder as soon as she was certain Mrs. Killington wasn't looking her way.

Afterward, she immediately regretted it. Her heart banged painfully against her ribs. She was drenched in a flash flood of perspiration. Oh, God, *why* had she done such a stupid thing? *What* could have gotten into her?

She watched Len's head, with its almond-colored swirls of hair, bent over his desk as he read the note. She waited, breath held, for him to turn around. To wink, or maybe whisper something.

He didn't.

Instead, he picked up his pencil and completed his quiz without so much as a glance in her direction. Ashley did the same, but her heart wasn't in it. Why didn't Len turn around and give her a sign?

Ashley quickly checked over her answers, then fixed her gaze on the big clock on the wall over the blackboard. The second hand swept around and around. The minute hand would be still for the longest time, then leap forward suddenly with a loud click.

Five minutes passed before Len made a move.

Ashley's heart came to a screeching halt as Len rose, stretched his arms leisurely overhead, scratched his shoulder, then strode to the front of the class and dropped his test paper on Mrs. Killington's desk. He didn't look back.

It's hopeless, Ashley thought, a queasy, sick feeling in the pit of her stomach. I've made a total jerk of myself again.

At that moment the bell rang.

Ashley made a dash for the corridor. She felt as if she'd suddenly been stripped of all her clothes. Len knew how she felt about him now. Her heart might as well be carved into a tree trunk, with hers and Len's initials in it.

But Len had ignored her note.

He was probably laughing at her right now.

Ashley risked a sneaked glance over her shoulder.

Len was right behind her . . . with Alicia Sanchez at his side.

Now I know why they call it a crush when you fall in

162

love with someone, Ashley thought miserably. Because you feel as if your heart's been run over by a steam roller.

The baseball diamond was deserted when she arrived at the end of the school day. She had expected it to be. After all, there was no reason in the world why Len should be here, was there?

Still, she hadn't been able to keep from harboring the tiniest spark of hope on her walk to the field. Now the spark was smothered, leaving a hollow ache in her chest as she sank down on the bottom riser of the bleachers, staring out at the empty space with its scruffy grass, balding in patches where countless players had slid into the bases.

Len is probably taking Alicia to the Homecoming Dance, she thought.

And I'll end up staying home that night. I'll bake chocolate-chip cookies, and eat half the batter, and make myself sick. Then I'll watch a sad movie on the late show, and cry into my pillow . . .

The wind rose, rattling through the maple trees on the other side of the cyclone fence that bordered the field. A handful of gold- and flame-colored leaves swirled through the air, as if performing some graceful ballet. One bright scarlet leaf landed on the grass at Ashley's feet. She picked it up, twirling it between her fingers. Then, closing her stinging eyes, she brushed it gently along her cheek.

"Yo . . . Ashley." A deep voice startled her. Was she imagining it? Could it be—

Her eyes flew open. "Len!"

He stood before her, his weight shifting onto one leg, his thumbs hooked through the frayed belt loops of his jeans. He was staring straight at her with those sleepy-lidded, gold green eyes, making her feel flushed and shivery, all at once.

"I got your note," he said with a huskiness that rippled through her. "How come you ran away after class?"

Ashley stared at him, feeling like a fish jerked suddenly from the water. "I . . . I thought . . . well, that is . . ." She gulped. "I thought you weren't interested in meeting me."

Len just looked at her, and shook his head. *"You* thought *I* wouldn't be interested? That's funny, because *you're* the one who's always running away. I figured it was me. You just didn't like me, or something."

Ashley couldn't believe what she was hearing. Could Len have possibly had the same kinds of doubts she had? Is that why he hadn't turned around in class? It didn't seem possible. And yet . . .

"Why wouldn't I like you?" she asked in amazement.

Len shrugged and looked down at the scuffed toe of his boot as he drew a circle with it in the dirt next to Ashley's feet. "All kinds of reasons. Like, you know, I'm this tough guy from the big city, and you . . . well, you're like some kind of princess. Your father owns the company. My father just works there. I figured you might be ashamed to be seen with me."

Ashley shook her head. "Oh, Len . . ." She couldn't find the words to tell him how wrong he was.

"That day at the picnic," Len continued, "I was glad we finally got to talk, because . . . well, you know, I'd been wanting to get to know you, and all. Then you backed off all of a sudden, like you wanted me to get lost." He looked up at her, his green gold eyes blazing. "When I got your note today in Mrs. K.'s class, I thought you might be playing some kind of joke on me. You know, like cat and mouse. But I came, anyway. I had to find out for sure."

Ashley felt like a leaf dancing in midair, swirling, dipping, light as the wind.

"I thought . . . well, you and Alicia seemed to be spending a lot of time together," she said hesitantly.

"Alicia? Yeah, she hangs around sometimes. But we're just friends." He broke out in a sheepish grin. "Well, okay, so maybe she'd like to be more than just friends.

164

But she's not really my type." He dropped down beside her on the bench, gently brushing back a strand of hair that was blowing across her cheek. "I have this thing for redheads, you see."

Ashley began to relax. Len wasn't so hard to talk to. Maybe they weren't so different, after all. Her skin tingled where he'd touched her. "Even klutzy redheads?" she asked.

Len laughed. "You, a klutz? Come on. When I saw you sliding home that day in the classroom, well, old Reggie couldn't have done it better himself. So I figured I'd better get to know you before the Red Sox or the Giants snapped you up."

"Who, me? I can't even throw a baseball straight. That's why I didn't want to play on your team at the picnic. I wasn't backing off. I was just embarrassed."

"Baseball's easy. C'mon, I'll show you." Len fished a ball from the pocket of his windbreaker. "Your note said you'd changed your mind, so I came prepared."

As Ashley walked beside Len out onto the diamond, a warm glow spread through her. The grass seemed to unroll before her like a magic carpet—one that would take her anywhere she wanted to go. Or let her be whoever she wanted to be.

Someday maybe she would go back in time again, to Ancient Egypt perhaps, or Imperial China. She'd scale a pyramid or visit an emperor's court. Or flirt with a pharaoh.

But right now the only place she wanted to be was right here on this scruffy old field. With Len.

And the only person she wanted to be was herself. Plain old Ashley Calhoun.

Len placed the ball in her palm, curving his big hand about her knuckles. "You hold it like this," he murmured. "And throw it like this . . ." He positioned himself at her back, guiding her arm in a slow-motion pitch. She could feel the warm flutter of his breath against her ear. His nylon windbreaker whispered against her clothing. "See, it's not so hard. By the way,'' he added casually, ''what are you doing the night of the Homecoming Dance?''

Time stood still. For Ashley, there could never be anything more perfect than this moment.

''Nothing,'' she said, tossing the ball into the air and watching it fly in a perfect spinning arc across the denim-colored sky.

AVON FLARE ◆ NOVELS
FROM BESTSELLING AUTHOR
MARILYN SACHS

FOURTEEN   69842-0/$2.50 US/$2.95 Can

Rebecca's mother has just finished her fourteenth book. They'd all been about Rebecca. Each time her mother promised the main character would not resemble her, and each time she was recognized. This time Mrs. Cooper thought she had played it safe by writing *First Love*, a typical teenage romance. But that was before Jason moved next door.

CLASS PICTURES   61408-1/$2.50 US/$2.95 Can

When shy, plump Lolly Scheiner arrives in kindergarten, she is the "new girl everyone hates," and only popular Pat Maddox jumps to her defense. From then on they're best friends through thick and thin, supporting each other during crises until everything changes in eighth grade, when Lolly suddenly turns into a thin pretty blonde and Pat, an introspective science whiz, finds herself playing second fiddle for the first time.